RISING
A SINFUL SOLDIER ROMANCE

LEXXI JAMES

To first responders everywhere. Our true heroes.

1

KATHRYN

"Naked? Where?" the receptionist asked, giddy as she spoke into her cell.

Kathryn warmed with a smile. These were the moments she lived for. That brief sliver of time when she could hear every word of someone's private conversation and they hadn't the vaguest clue she was there, standing roughly three feet away.

She hadn't exactly snuck up on the woman, but the carpeting softened her steps. Listening in, this was most of her life with Wolfe Investigations, day in and day out. Eavesdropping. Snooping. Call it what you will, but it was her God-given gift. The life she was born for.

"How naked?" The receptionist, whose name was Celeste according to her nameplate, asked this question because obviously there were varying degrees of nudity. Especially when referring to a twenty-year-old young man at his grandparents' vow renewal.

Silently, Kathryn craned her body, twisting it just enough to catch every descriptive and tattooed detail.

"Oh!" Celeste said, freezing midspin in her chair when she caught sight of Kathryn. "I'll call you back," she whispered, her rosy cheeks brightening as she disconnected and tucked the phone behind her.

Before Kathryn could introduce herself, Celeste popped to her feet. "Let me just see if he's ready for you."

"Thank you."

The young woman bolted down the long hall and returned a few moments later. "He said he'll be right with you. And so, so sorry about earlier." The poor girl gushed out an apology, prayer hands and all.

"Thank you, and no need to be sorry." Kathryn leaned over. "How naked was he?"

Celeste unleashed, spilling every last drop of tea. "It wasn't just that he was naked—which he totally was. Or that he was caught in the honeymoon suite—aka, Papaw and Memaw's bedroom. It was that he was with the caterer . . . and not his date. Who happens to be my cousin. Men," Celeste said with a huff, "are asses."

"Not all of them," Kathryn said knowingly as her thumb brushed the diamond ring on her finger.

Turning, she surveyed the available seats in the waiting room. The man wearing the decent suit wielding a rollaway suitcase was probably a pharmaceutical rep. Notorious talkers.

Pass.

And the three others were medical personnel—two nurses and a doctor—each studying their own notes and didn't need to be disturbed. She found a quiet corner as "Hot Stuff" by Donna Summer blared from her purse. The smarmy salesman nodded in approval.

She dug her phone from her purse and answered, scrunching her face in apology to the three stoic professionals as she plopped her derriere into the nearest seat.

Sliding in her earbuds, she whispered, "Hi."

"If this is your phone-sex voice, my credit card number is ready."

Kathryn tried to hold back the giggle Jake always had a way of dragging from her at the worst possible times.

"Busy?" he asked.

"About to be," she said with regret, pressing her thighs together as his gruff voice did its usual number on her system. "I miss you."

"How much do you miss me?" It was easy to imagine Jake's lips smiling through fourteen full days of stubble as his suggestive question lingered in her ear.

Crossing her legs and battling her rising heat, she said, "More than I can say at the moment."

His FaceTime request was instant. She accepted, expecting the man who'd been working around the clock in who knows what country to look downright exhausted.

What was she thinking? This was Jake Russo. The man with ceaseless energy and a libido to match. And right now, Jake was all of those things and soaking wet on top of it.

Fresh out of the shower, the man was a god with his hair dripping and body slick with lickable droplets he deliberately avoided drying off. He was either making a strong case for phone sex, or running to his Thunder from Down Under audition.

"And what are you doing at this moment?" he asked, teasing her with glimpses down his chest.

"An interview," she said effortlessly because it was kinda-sorta true. It was an interview. Just not the sort of interview usually required by her job, putting Kathryn across the table from witnesses and suspects alike, gathering their statements to paint a picture of the truth.

No, this time, she was massaging the truth, taking an interview for a job she hadn't asked for, for a position she couldn't help wanting. It was the kind of work she'd run circles around others doing, so why were her palms sweating?

Maybe because Jake was panning his phone's camera downward.

She let out a gasp and sank into her seat, tapping each earbud in securely to ensure absolute privacy in a room of strangers. "What, um, time are you returning?"

"Home? Around four tomorrow afternoon. But sooner if I can."

She latched onto the word *home*. "So, you'll be in Colorado before that?"

The extra-long pause he took to answer the question wasn't nearly as suspicious as the slight tightening of his jaw, producing his "angry" dimple.

Oh my gosh. Can he be here now?

Finally, he answered. "A quick trip to Boulder. But back by four. So, ready to see how much I miss you?" He tipped the camera again, giving her glimpses of the ridges in the muscles along his abs and hips.

Battling between grilling him further about where he was and outright licking the screen, Kathryn jolted from her chair when someone touched her shoulder. She fumbled her phone and caught it in midair, snapping it to her chest.

"Excuse me," the receptionist said apologetically. "He's ready for you, Mrs. Reeves."

Kathryn collected herself, controlling her breaths.

Jake was in her ear. "Did she say Mrs. Reeves? Undercover?"

"No," she said honestly. Standing, she nodded to the young woman, smiling sweetly as she said to her, "I'm Kathryn Chase."

"Oh. Okay, Ms. Chase. This way."

The petite woman led her down a long hall.

"I'll call you back," Kathryn murmured at her phone, pushing out her bottom lip in deflated protest.

"Then I'll take care of that perfect pout tomorrow. Love you."

The receptionist opened a glass door with the words DIVISION CHAIR - SURGICAL SPECIALITIES etched into the glass, giving Kathryn access to an office overlooking the mountain range in the distance, and the towering man before her. Hands on his hips, it was clear she was keeping him waiting a millisecond too long.

"I love you too," she whispered into the phone and disconnected the call.

"And you're about to love me too," the Chief of Surgery said, his white physician coat looking way too starched and pressed to be practical.

Ten bucks says he had his socks ironed. And probably his underwear.

Kathryn huffed, doing her best to keep her eye roll to a minimum.

"I'll just bet. Why did your receptionist call me Mrs. Reeves?" Straightening her stance, she asked, "I thought you invited me here for an interview."

With a stern glance that instantly had her sitting down opposite him, he didn't mince words. "Come on, Kat—"

"Kathryn," she said quickly, correcting him.

"Fine, Kathryn," he said, stressing her full given name for effect. And because he was an ass. "Whatever my secretary said was her mistake, not mine. And we both know the interview was just a ruse to get you here. I sent you everything I have. The job is yours if you want it. We'll build as we go. Full autonomy. You can name your price. All I want from you is a yes or a no."

No would be the prudent answer. There were so many things that could go wrong with this arrangement, such as the amount of work. And the proximity to the narcissistic face of Mr. Fucking Perfect. Aka, her new boss.

Oh yeah. And her ex-husband.

Dr. Carter Reeves was a brilliant surgeon. Avid golfer, skier, and mountain climber. And newly appointed hospital department chair, hence his recent return to Colorado. And the reason his arrogant grin anticipated her response before she even gave it.

"Yes." Kathryn beamed before she could stop herself. Before that pivotal moment when her brain engaged and kicked her in the ass, and a small knot formed in her gut. *This is such a bad idea.*

Schooling her emotions, she said, "I mean maybe. A test drive to see how it goes. But I don't want people knowing it was you who did this."

The handsome man arched that perfectly thick brow, a move that should be illegal. One that had charmed Kathryn endless times in the past, but that was ancient history. He'd always been just *this* close to being the total package. And then he'd open his mouth.

He smirked. "You mean you don't want Jake to know?"

And there it was. The arrogance that made this total package intolerable.

Of course it would be too much to expect him not to know about Jake. He was rich. Connected. And there was that whole Facebook-friend thing he and Kathryn still had going on. Technically, his profile was snoozed every thirty days, but he didn't need to know that.

"I'm not hiding it from Jake." *Exactly.* "I'm just compartmentalizing certain things." *Like my man and you.* "I'm just trying something new."

"No explanation needed," he said, hardly modest with his smug-as-shit grin that always managed to sprout a dimple. "And if you were test-driving that line on me, it sounds great."

The wink? Equally as irritating. *I hate myself for laughing.*

True, it wouldn't be every day, so Jake might not notice right away. Because it wasn't like her fiancé was one of the leading investigators in the world. In cyber investigations, no less. Jake was more than brilliant at his work and in demand worldwide. Her husband-to-be was a damned bloodhound.

But trying to snow Jake Russo even for a second?

I am so earning a punishment.

Besides, if Jake was anything, he was a raging workaholic. Lately, he was out of town more than he was home. Not that Kathryn was necessarily complaining.

Have I burned the midnight oil time and time again? Guilty.

In total disgrace, she hadn't even let half a second go by before she blurted, "When do I start?"

My hardball could use some serious work.

"Is tomorrow too soon? Two o'clock?" Carter asked.

"Two's perfect." *I'll squeeze it in before Jake returns. What can go wrong?*

"Then it's a date."

I'm not going to argue with the pompous schmo who just offered me the chance to explore my dream job, but I'm mentally throwing out there that this is not a date.

"And now that I've done you a favor, Nurse Chase, I need you to do me one."

The title instantly tickled Kathryn's soul, resulting in a poorly hidden cheesy grin. "Anything."

"A chance to catch up," Carter said, which wouldn't be overly concerning until he added, "Over dinner."

"Dinner?" she squeaked out.

"I promise, nothing fancy." *Shocker.* "And I won't take no for an answer."

2
KATHRYN

Knock-knock.

Kathryn had a need to escape, shed her guilt, and visit a friend. This detour hit all three. Knocking was a deeply ingrained courtesy, and the only way to avoid possibly seeing a naked man on the other side of a hospital room door.

Without waiting for an answer, Kathryn pushed open the door and made her way in. "Everyone decent?" she asked, double-checking just in case.

"Not hardly." Detective Scott Delaney was his usual ex-military self, his naturally perfect posture evident even as he was laid up in a bed with one leg in a cast. Smiling, he set down the newspaper, letting Kathryn catch a glance at his sudoku block.

"Eight," she said, pointing to the third square.

He narrowed his eyes, unamused until he glanced at the page. After scribbling an eight into the block in question, he tucked the paper away. "Kathryn, what, uh, are you doing here?"

"Madeline said you were in the hospital. With her in the middle of depositions all day, and Jake out of town, I was in the area and had nothing better to do with my time than engage in a little freelance stalking."

She'd barely uttered her last word when a Styrofoam cup of water fell to the floor, spilling across the tile. It was then that Kathryn noticed the man in the other bed. The nurse in her was ready to swoop in and collect it, stopped by an insistent grab of her arm. Scott's grip wasn't exactly gentle. The patient was practically twice her size, but his subtle wince was noticeable.

"Kathryn," he said a little louder than necessary, considering the size of the room, "meet my bunkmate, Troy. Troy, Kathryn is a good friend. An investigator."

The small shakiness of Troy's hand stilled as he balled it to a controlled fist. Nodding, he lifted a brow. "Private investigator?" he asked, almost sounding hopeful.

Flattered, she shook her head. "I'm into the high-adrenaline world of insurance fraud," she joked, and yet Troy's lips remained in a straight line. *Tough crowd.* "In for bad behavior like this one?" Kathryn asked, thumping the cast on Scott's leg. The hollow sound drew her attention, and she gave it a second glance.

"Something like that," Troy said, grumbling the words low.

There was a strange familiarity to the rough lines of his face, his high cheekbones and dark brown eyes. But it was the pensive faraway stare Kathryn recognized most. Despite Troy's impressive build and stoic brow, worry bled through his expression like watercolor across paper. A likely consequence of whatever medical procedure he had coming.

Three loud knocks and the door again opened wide, this time to allow two men to enter, one rolling a gurney.

They began the usual drill, asking Troy to confirm his date of birth and compared it to his wristband, which meant he was probably heading for imaging or surgery. They asked about the procedure he'd be having. Another failsafe of the system to confirm the right guy gets the right procedure, and not an unnecessary appendectomy. Or vasectomy.

Respecting the man's privacy, Kathryn slipped out into the hall, but not entirely out of earshot. Apparently, Troy was getting a knee replacement.

She knew it well. Take a standard-issue soldier, add thirty pounds of body armor, strap a hundred more pounds of equipment to his or her back, then send them on a ten-mile hike. Voilà. Instant knee demolition.

As the gurney was pushed out of the room, she caught Troy's pained expression.

"You'll be out before you know it," she said, followed by a comforting wink and a practiced smile, a natural reassurance she'd given to her own patients hundreds of times before.

Kathryn slipped back into the room and shut the door. "So?" she asked, popping an expectant brow, ready for Scott to give her the 411 on whatever was going on.

Scott hardened his expression. He pantomimed locking his lips, tossed the invisible key over his shoulder, and crossed his arms. Tightly.

Kathryn knew the drill. Fake cast. No chart at the end of the bed. The patient lying in bed before her wasn't her old pal Scott. Nope. This was Detective Delaney, and it was obvious he was undercover.

Instead of pestering Scott relentlessly like she normally would, threatening to expose his secret love of *The Bachelor*, or making his life a living hell by relentlessly tickling his foot below the fake cast, she plopped her butt on the bed, fully prepared to engage in whatever idle chitchat would relieve him from his boredom. Because faking disinterest is definitely a superpower.

"All right, all right, I give." Scott's hands flew up in surrender. For a guy used to grilling insidious masterminds and hard-core criminals alike, he cracked like a walnut. "I'm on a case. Protecting Troy Brooks from a stalker."

Wide-eyed, Kathryn leaned in and lowered her voice. "That was Troy Brooks? Pro basketball point guard? Don't tell Julian, or the poor man will have two stalkers. Isn't he dating supermodel Alexis Kennedy?"

"He was. With everything that's been happening, they publicly called it off. Privately, he's got a bodyguard covering her around the clock."

"And you? Is this you moonlighting?"

"If only. Then maybe Madeline would get that trip to Turks and Caicos she's always wanted. His stalker is guilty of a dozen crimes, and is always one goddamned step ahead of us."

Curious, Kathryn had to know. "What happened to his knee?"

Scott shook his head with regret. "We offered assistance and gave him tons of solid advice, but men are the worst victims. Precautions fly out the window because they believe women aren't a threat. The psycho chick who shot him in the leg was actually trying to kidnap him."

"Nothing says love like Stockholm Syndrome."

Not wanting to waste a perfectly good Sharpie, Kathryn picked it up from the nightstand and began doodling on Scott's cast. The resin wasn't exactly taking to the ink like it should, but that's the great thing about Sharpies. They mark anything.

"Careful." Scott jolted, lowering his voice. "That cast is hiding a gun."

She settled him back with a smartass grin. "Oh, I'll be gentle. Tell me everything. Doodling helps me think."

Scott relaxed into the fluffy pillows at his back. "His stalker had him at gunpoint, and Troy went for the gun. Frankly, he's lucky to be alive. And this was the second attempt. First time, his sports drink had been laced with sedatives. She was halfway through tying him up when he came to."

"At least he has you," Kathryn said while doodling flowers around the phrase YOGA KICKED MY ASS.

"But it's not over. Twice now, we've intercepted notes coming to his room. This is the third time we've had to move him in twenty-four hours."

Scott's stare weighed on her but she paid it no mind, keeping herself dutifully immersed in scrawling the phrase, when your wife is vacuuming and says move your feet, you should listen!

By the time she'd finished drawing the fifth heart around it, she couldn't keep ignoring his persistent stare. "What?"

"You're perfect."

Suspicious, she gave him a sideways glance. "Funny, you don't look like Jake."

"No, I mean for this job. You're a top-notch investigator who knows your way around a hospital. We need someone who can observe things unnoticed. Like I said, you're perfect."

"You can't bribe me with flattery, Scott. The minimum buy-in is booze and a plate of Madeline's pecan-chocolate-chip cookies."

"Done and done."

"I'd like to help you out, but I'm already beyond swamped." Shyly, Kathryn said, "I'm considering a career change . . ."

3
KATHRYN

"*D*id I hear something about a career change?" Jake asked the next day in that deep, coaxing tone. Leave it to him to want to see her at the best—or possibly the worst time ever.

He'd just gotten back into town and showed up at the hospital, surprising her. Not only was he earlier than expected, but he'd somehow managed to hear about her job and track her down.

Curse that phone finder. And leave it to Jake's ole pal Scott to spill the beans. For a detective, Scott spreads news faster than Twitter.

Good luck finding that remote, buddy.

It was hard enough resisting Jake's boyish grin, rugged jaw, and delectable lips. But those darkening hazel eyes always did Kathryn in. It was as if they existed just to expose every last secret hidden deep within her.

But she wasn't ready to share this one. Not yet.

What if I don't like it? What if it's just one of a dozen things I try? What if it means working less and less with Jake?

Leave it to him to want to see her at the best—or possibly the worst time ever. He'd just gotten back into town and here he is. Not only was he earlier than expected, but he'd tracked her down.

Curse that phone finder.

Kathryn checked her watch. Five minutes before she had to start. "Change might be too strong a word. More of an add-on."

"Like whipped cream?"

This man will be the death of me.

It wasn't just that her thumping pulse was making it hard to concentrate, or that that sensual rumble to his voice always lit a match right between her legs. It was the heat it evoked, that slow burn rising steadily up her neck and cheeks that meant every stranger in this class would see right through her.

"There's that beautiful blush I live for," he said a little loudly as two nurses walked past them.

Timidly, Kathryn smiled. Her reaction to the sight of him rippled through her body, the slow burn of lava landing straight at her core. His dark T-shirt exposed every cut of his arms and his lickable tattoos, and his jeans presented themselves in a way that demanded removal. Stat.

The second his hand cradled her neck and his lips lowered to hers, it was over. Each slow pass of his mouth against hers was torture and ownership. Jake was lust incarnate.

And I. Can't. Breathe.

His strong arms wrapped around her were all that were holding her up.

"Phlebotomy?" he asked.

Her body tensed, giving her the strength to stand up straight. "What?"

How did he—

Jake pivoted her body just enough to see the words written across the whiteboard hanging on the door next to them. WELCOME TO BASICS OF PHLEBOTOMY.

"Heading to class, Nurse Chase?" he asked.

She cleared her throat. "Teaching, actually. It's just a trial run," she said modestly, circling a finger along his chest but not meeting his gaze.

Two fingers lifted her chin. "I have a feeling you're going to love it."

"The phone-finder app got you to the hospital. But how did you know I was here exactly?"

"I have my ways." Jake's sexy half smile widened. "The spoils of working in cyber security. And using Google Alerts. It notified me that a very hot teacher was expected, which gave me just enough time to sign up."

"I'm on the internet?" That was fast. But then again, no one ever accused Carter Reeves of wasting time. *Wait.* "Did you say sign up?"

Confused, she watched as Jake fished something from his back pocket. This class was for entry-level medical personnel, mostly nursing students. All registered in one way or another with a medical practice or hospital.

As he retrieved a sticker and peeled it from its backing, she couldn't object. The man proudly slapped the nametag to his chest.

"EMT Russo reporting for class, ma'am."

A suspicious smile twisted on her face. This class was also offered to emergency medical technicians, both for newbies and those needing recertification. Jake's volunteer work with the local fire department depended on him keeping current.

"Your certification is due?"

"At the end of the year. Gotta go. Looks crowded, and I need to find a seat." Rushed, he left her with a quick peck before strolling in.

Sucking in a tense breath, Kathryn let it out and stalled to avoid waltzing in with him.

One-one-thousand. Two-one-thousand. An adequate amount of time to not announce to the entire world that her fiancé was in the class.

Said fiancé took a seat in the back, but still managed to lock eyes with her as she headed to the lectern at the front.

A binder was waiting for her. The YOU'LL DO GREAT! note was an unusually sweet gesture from Carter, one she rarely experienced when she'd worked for him, and never as his wife. After fanning through the two-hundred-page play-by-play that looked like someone had busily downloaded Wikipedia, Kathryn chalked it up as a waste of three perfectly good trees and chucked it aside.

"Welcome to Basics of Phlebotomy," she said. "I'm Kathryn Chase, and I'll be giving you life lessons in how to poke, prod, and make pincushions of fellow human beings. Or what I affectionately refer to as Vampire 101."

The mild laughter from her small audience was appreciated, but the goal was to get these nursing students to relax.

"Today, we're going over the basics. By the time we finish the course, you'll be able to draw blood, give injections, set up intravenous lines, and administer IV medications. Today's goal is pretty straightforward. Be as pain-free as possible as we stick each other."

It only took a breath before several hands shot up.

"On . . . each other?" Trepidation laced the voice of the student, and Kathryn smiled warmly at him.

"It's the best way to understand, because you'll be more careful on each other than you would a stranger. And no matter how small a needle is, it hurts. Add to that that the fear of needles is a top-ten American fear, affecting over one in six adults. This exercise helps us strengthen our need to heal with our bonds as people. When you give a shot, remember the very first requirement in a hospital is that we 'should do the sick no harm.'"

"Florence Nightingale," a tall, slender woman with jet-black hair announced from the back, recognizing the quote.

The woman sat in the seat next to Jake's, which allowed Kathryn to step a little closer. It also let her read the woman's nametag. *Andi*. Remembering each student's name before the end of today's lesson was Kathryn's goal.

Short dark hair. Brown eyes. Tallest girl in the room. Andi with an i.
Two down, twenty-eight to go.

"I'll go over a few techniques that will help you with the harder sticks, and then we'll pair off."

After going over the basic course content, as well as the tips and tricks for how to find a vein using Jake as her demonstration model, Kathryn let the teams get to work, encouraging them to move at a comfortable pace.

It was a proud moment when you nudged the little birds from the nest, then watched them jab each other in the arm and still meet each other's gaze with warm smiles and encouragement. It was how she and Julian had first met. Lifelong besties to this day.

The memory made her smile.

"Don't worry, Andi," Jake said, reassuring his partner as the color drained from her face. "I don't mind needles. Pain is my mistress. Go on. It'll be fine."

"Okay." Andi took several seconds finding just the right angle as Jake sent Kathryn a confident wink. Followed by a yelp.

Kathryn smothered a laugh, stepping in.

"Mistress troubles?" she asked, instantly recognizing the issue. "You're doing great. Ease back just a hair, Andi, but don't change angles or wiggle the needle. You've overshot the vein, but you can still salvage it without sticking him again."

Kathryn watched her protégé move through the steps. Jake's skeptical brow didn't go unnoticed, but Kathryn was confident. "Now try."

Andi drew the smallest amount of blood, keeping her grip steady as she squealed. "It worked."

"Now, go ahead and finish. What do you do next?"

Andi rattled off the steps. "Undo the tourniquet. Apply light pressure but don't fold the arm. Folding equals bruising."

"Great job." Kathryn scanned the progress of the other teams around the room and noted they were all wrapping up. "Nice work, everyone. See you in a few days."

She stood watching as her new students filed out of the room, waving good-bye to the last one. Except for Jake.

"A few days, huh?"

Jake's words feathered along the skin of her neck, a hum lingering in their wake. His finger barely brushed the underside of her ass as the students cleared out. "Can I offer you a lift, Teach?"

When she turned around to face him, his thumb glided against her full lower lip. It spent no time there, setting a gentle course across her blouse to the pucker of her nipple. Her head fell back until she remembered where they were, and her gaze snapped to the door.

No one there. Thank God. It would be just like Carter to drop by, though.

"Come on," Jake whispered, looping his arm around her waist.

It was a relief, them heading for the door. There, they stopped as he closed the door and locked it.

"I offered you a lift." His palm caressed the wall. "Right here should do."

Wide-eyed, Kathryn blinked for a good, long minute. "Here?"

Jake scooped her ass into the cradle of his arms. Her legs wrapped around him, completely betraying her better sense, because resisting this man? Not happening.

"Just giving you a little taste of things to come, kitten." The tug of his teeth on her earlobe ensured she was only picking up about half of whatever he was saying.

"*Hmm?*" She moaned, the hard press of his dick taunting her sex.

Her thighs widened. His zipper was down. And the skirt that six minutes ago was worn with a sense of professionalism and elegance could now be appreciated for its easy access. After two weeks of Kathryn and Jake being apart, nothing was keeping the thick, hard length of him from entering.

Nothing but several rattles of the doorknob, followed by an insistent *knock-knock-knock.*

"Crap. I think that's the next class wanting this room." Kathryn panted, dropping her head to his shoulder.

Jake's chuckle was warm against her neck. "Then I guess I'll give you the other kind of lift. Home."

"I'm pretty sure you drove here. Traffic from Boulder must have been nonexistent."

"Boulder?" he asked before quickly saying, "Yes. Boulder. No traffic at all."

He eased her feet to the floor, then hurried to tuck in his shirt and straighten his clothes. Kathryn followed suit in the hope no one could see *nearly had sex* written all over their appearance.

Kathryn opened the door, stone-faced and serious, greeting the small crowd of students who filed quickly into the class.

"There's got to be an empty room somewhere," she joked, but her scans up and down the hall caught the distinctive walk and charisma of a certain new department head. Whirling around, she whispered urgently to Jake, "Let's go home."

Growling, he narrowed his eyes. "Have you been good, kitten?"

With her ex heading straight for them, Kathryn said honestly, "No. I've been very, very bad."

Driving home separately, Kathryn pulled into the garage, trailing Jake by a few minutes at the most, even though the man had a lead foot.

But his absence when she walked inside was noticed. Jake not being there immediately to open her door, whisk her inside, and ravage her body relentlessly was unusual.

And after two weeks apart, it was inconceivable.

Unless, he had a surprise waiting. More than likely, she'd be walking into a fragrant sea of dozens of roses, champagne, and chocolate-covered strawberries.

Maybe it was time she gave him a little surprise of her own for once. And as she had to walk in on her own two feet, she might as well make the most of it.

It only took her a second to peel away her clothes, tug off her ponytail holder, and tousle her hair for that perfect *please, for the love of God, fuck me already* look.

Confident, she smiled wide and breezed inside. "Jake?"

Jake's gaze swept over her body, and he bolted up and rushed between naked-as-a-jaybird Kathryn and Armani-clad Paco Robles, the right-hand man to Alex Drake, CEO of Drake Global Industries.

Simultaneously, Kathryn and Paco screamed in horror, though it could be argued that Paco's scream was an octave higher. Paco was a powerful man whose friendship with Kathryn was debatably longer than it was with Jake, though both bonds were equally as strong.

"Look, baby," Jake said with a forced smile. "Paco decided to surprise us since he knew I'd be returning to town today."

Nothing spelled suspicious like Jake calling her *baby*. It was actually the first time Jake had ever referred to Kathryn as *baby*, which reeked of code, some little hint-hint between the two men. But looking Paco up and down, Kathryn decided there was no way it was bro code.

Jake hiding a lover? Ridiculous. Paco was her *ride or die*. As evidenced by him handing Jake his blazer to wrap Kathryn in. So, she filed it under *further research* and moved on.

Secondly, Kathryn already suspected that Jake had been in town for the past two weeks, rather than out of town as he'd said. Which was fine. There were times in their work they couldn't divulge super-secret stuff like missions and whereabouts to each other. In Jake's work, national interests might be at stake, which was fair enough. But that would mean that Paco was there for something else.

Whatever the reason, at the very moment, it didn't matter.

"Paco," Kathryn said, shyly remaining behind Jake. "It's great to see you, but no call or text is unusual."

"I call it impulsive."

"How long are you in town?"

"A . . . few days."

Why does his statement sound more like a question? And what was with the uncertain glance at Jake?

Before Kathryn could ask with her outside voice, Jake jumped in.

"I think what Kathryn's subtly trying to say is we love you, but unless it's urgent—"

"It's not," Paco said, already headed toward the door to make his way out.

"Wait," Kathryn said. "You dropped by, and you always have an agenda when you drop by."

"You're so suspicious," Paco said, stalling.

"I'm always right," Kathryn said, knotting the oversized sleeves and crossing her arms in a knowing stance.

Paco exchanged a glance with Jake before replying. "You're right.

My room key is in that jacket. Bring them both to the Broadmoor tomorrow. Spa day, just you and me. I'll text you the time."

Squealing, she lost all interest in grilling Father Christmas and accepted.

Having deposited a wonderful gift, Paco was out the door, giving Jake the freedom to whisk Kathryn against his chest and take two stairs at a time on their way to the bedroom.

"I thought he would never leave," Jake said.

Before Kathryn could ask any one of the dozen questions she had about what had just happened, Jake's lips were on hers, crushing her mouth in dominant desire. His kiss was impatient and demanding, his rough bristles burning needy tracks along her mouth and neck, his fingers smoothing the blazer from her shoulders.

Jake didn't say a word, letting Kathryn strip his clothes away and massage across the muscles of his chest, down the granite features of his abs, tracing along the sexy *V* of his thighs until her hands were heavy with the thickness of his cock.

Hauling her body to his, Jake had her settled into position centered on the bed, her thighs spread to welcome him. Under the intensity of his gaze, any curiosities and doubts dissipated, leaving only room for Jake.

With a last deep kiss along her lips, his head moved down, dipping between her legs, rough stubbled nips along her inner thighs, and soothing hungry licks that were too close to undoing her.

"Jake," she whimpered, but he wasn't stopping.

Desperate, she gripped his hair, scraped his back and neck, and rocked her hips to the rhythm of each hungry, invasive lick. Each perfect touch. Chasing a climax that shredded her utterly and completely apart.

Two weeks without him, and it wasn't enough.

Her orgasm went on and on as he nipped and lapped, sucked and licked her swollen pussy and sensitive clit. But it was his finger, pressing inside and gliding in long strokes to coax another wave of pleasure. One more long, hard lick was all it took.

"Now, kitten," he demanded.

Her body gave in harder and faster than the first time, like the eternity of fourteen days crashed in wave upon wave of want and desire. Shuddering, her breaths were frantic, each breath out a shaky, fragile gasp.

"Jake."

As he moved up her body, each kiss reminded her how much she loved him. Her fingers always found the scars across his torso, dusting them with the lightest touch. Knowing he was hers. His bristles teased along the tight peak of her nipple, and the heat of his thick head barely slid to the entrance of her core when she bucked forward.

Jake pulled away, leaving Kathryn in a heaving pile of moans and sighs.

"You said you've been very, very bad. I'll be taking my time with your sweet pussy."

His smug grin had her thrusting again, aching for a cock he was keeping just out of reach.

"The technical term is murder," she teased, panting her words. "And it's not like I'm the only one."

His half smile was delicious, even more so when it was covering her mouth. He moved away quickly, avoiding her accusatory smirk, intent on distracting her. His teeth were punishing as he grazed one nipple and pinched another. With the tip of his cock in position, he worked his thick hardness in, gliding up and down her walls, filling her before dragging himself out.

With Jake determined to blissfully torture her to death, she had no choice but to take every inch however he chose to give it to her. It didn't last. Within a few thrusts, he plunged deeper, harder, forcing her legs wider, crashing into her until his cries drowned out her own.

When his body finally collapsed on hers and his thundering heartbeat gentled, she heard the only words that jolted her already frantic pulse.

"I love you, kitten. My future wife."

4

KATHRYN

"This is amazing," Kathryn gushed to her friend the next afternoon, the one with the movie-star good looks and a smile that was natural and effortless. "Fancy hotel. Spa day. No wonder I'm always ecstatic to see you. But why do I feel like you're trying to butter me up?"

"Don't be silly. The spa day is for me," Paco said, the lie absolutely adorable. "And since we could connect—two birds, one stone."

But even with his plush chair reclined and eye mask on, Kathryn could see the tension Paco Robles' perfect body held, from the tense line of his jaw to the vein that seemed ready to burst from his silky-smooth forehead.

"It must be tough, being one of the most powerful and influential men in the world."

With all the responsibilities Paco carried on his muscular shoulders, it was clear that a few hours' reprieve was as close to a day off as he probably ever got.

"It has its perks," he murmured.

That was clear as she admired the beautiful Colorado wilderness from the setting of Paco's penthouse suite, whose luxury furnishings and gilded fixtures easily rivaled those of Versailles, but that wasn't the only similarity. Kathryn and Paco shared their intimate spa day with a butler, two manicurists, a chef, and two masseuses waiting in the wings. It was just how the man rolled.

But the two security guards sporting massive concealed weapons beneath their tailored suits might have been overkill. Or, the only way he could let his guard down and relax.

Their presence made Kathryn wonder. Paco wasn't a worrier, and he never overreacted. Whatever he was dealing with, she hoped he knew he didn't have to work it out alone. Instinctively, she placed a reassuring hand over his, careful not to smudge his fresh coat of clear polish.

In their plush robes and with drinks in hand, Kathryn might have been tipsier than usual. Trying to keep up with a man whose liver kicked into overtime around three in the afternoon was a tough job, but someone had to do it.

"Another round," he called out, lifting a hand in the air.

See? Tough job.

The butler refreshed his glass before topping off her flute of champagne. Kathryn quickly sipped the brut, smiling as the bubbles tickled her nose. Unmoved, Paco simply lay there.

"Want to talk about it?"

The subtle shake of his head was enough. She let it go, but not before adding, "If you need anything, I'm here for you."

He seemed to acknowledge her offer with a small nod, but said nothing else. Usually a chatterbox, Paco being this quiet was unnerving.

After taking another sip, Kathryn asked, "What's it like?"

"What's what like?" Paco lifted just enough of his mask to peek at her. His confusion looked entirely unnatural on him, making her giggle before she could get the words out.

"Oh, you know. Being a Dom." She smiled, making the right sort of small talk that achieved its intended effect, replacing the tightness of his jaw with an inescapable grin.

The charming smile turned mischievous, curling with naughty

intrigue. Removing his mask and tossing it aside, Paco popped that playful brow. The one that somehow managed to make the man clad in a ten-thousand-dollar suit seem sweet and approachable.

It's not like Paco Robles was just another rich, handsome man with dangerous good looks and a body of toned muscles and two-percent body fat. And he wasn't just another friend. He was Kathryn's confidant, someone she'd half recklessly approached to be her Dom, because why not? He was gay, safe, and would carry that secret to the grave.

Fortunately for both of them, he'd declined, thrusting her into the path of the Dom who stole her heart. Jake. Thankfully, there was no lingering awkwardness between Kathryn and Paco. If anything, the experience had bonded them as friends. Friends with fetishes.

When the manicurist giggled, Paco's stern words in what must have been her native language caused her to snort. "Keep massaging while you laugh," he said, pointing a commanding finger straight at his feet.

"What did you say to them?" Kathryn asked softly, filled with curiosity.

"I reminded her that she can't believe everything she hears about me. And that she's not as innocent as she looks."

The woman ducked her head, but there was no hiding her smile as she kneaded Paco's pretty foot. Kathryn took a woeful look at her own Barney Rubble feet and sighed.

"At least Jake's not a foot-fetish guy."

"Maybe he will be when he sees how gorgeous those piggies look." Paco held his glass to hers, inviting a toast. "To you and your journey down the BDSM brick road to the wonderful dungeon of Oz."

"I'll drink to that," she said, and after they'd clinked glasses, she took a refreshing sip. "*Mmm*, this is so good." Kathryn leaned back into her chair, allowing her mind to drift, trying to forget about how she'd tracked Jake's phone earlier.

"So," Paco said playfully as he sat back into his seat, his muscles now relaxed as his salacious grin worked overtime. "What makes you think I'm a Dom?"

"Well, you're sure as hell not a sub," she said, eliciting another round of delighted giggles from the girls tending to their feet.

"Maybe . . ." Paco stretched out the word, looking at each of the girls before turning to Kathryn. "I'm a switch."

Kathryn nearly snorted a little of the expensive champagne straight out her nose. The thought of big bad Paco being a Dom one minute, then taking a flogging on the ass the next, was definitely a visual she hadn't considered. And now, staring hard at him, she couldn't tell if he was yanking her chain or possibly swung both ways.

"Is there such a thing?" she asked.

Paco relaxed back, beaming with a suggestive smile. "Welcome to the world of infinite possibilities. Anything—and I do mean *anything*—goes." He sat up, releasing a string of exotic-sounding words that made both women scurry away.

Kathryn looked at her unpainted toes—all six of them. "Are they done?" she asked, half ready to reach for the polish and quickly finish the job herself before she and Paco moved on to their massages.

"No. I sent them away for a moment. Now, what do you really want to ask?"

Damn if that man didn't always have a way of getting to the point.

Kathryn stammered through starting and stopping what she wanted to say. Paco waited patiently, letting her decide when the silence between them would be broken by her questions. Her worries.

"Jake hasn't—"

"Stop," Paco said firmly, holding up a freshly manicured hand. "As much as I love you, Kathryn, and would do just about anything for you, I still have to work with the man. I'd prefer not to carry mental images of him in a random assortment of creative positions."

"No positions will be disclosed," Kathryn said quickly. "It's just that Jake hasn't taken me—"

"Jake Russo hasn't taken you?" Paco winked. "The man is seriously slipping."

Kathryn frowned. "He hasn't taken me . . . you know . . . out."

"Out?" Paco said slowly.

"To a club. A BDSM club." Her words came out somber and concerned. Hearing them aloud, she downed the rest of her bubbly, eager to swallow her ingratitude and silliness.

"Why aren't you having this conversation with Jake? Communication, especially in this world, is important. As much as there is no judgment, there are also no assumptions."

"Full disclosure? Because I think he's keeping things from me. Secrets."

"Hey," Paco said, coaxing her gaze. "We all keep secrets. Even me. Even you." He touched a finger to her nose.

Paco was right. When you worked in investigations, secrecy came with the territory. But this was different.

"Jake's going to clubs without me."

Paco set down his drink, studying Kathryn with a skeptical look. "What makes you say that?"

"Because he's been going to them when he's supposed to be away," Kathryn said, deflating as she added, "In Boulder."

"Boulder." Paco echoed her, the doubt clearly written across his flawless brow. "The obvious hot spot of frisky business."

Kathryn narrowed her eyes. "Fine. Let's see where he is now."

"Kathr—"

"*Tut-tut!*" Manicured hand in his face, she picked up her phone, careful of her freshly painted nails, and clicked on the phone-finder app. When the little pin popped up, she showed it to Paco. "Hmm, what's this? He's at one now."

And there it was. That devilish grin of Paco's that couldn't be masked.

He enjoyed a long sip of his champagne, draining his glass. Like the loyal friend he was, he said nothing, letting a slow *hmm* hit the air, the *you don't say* clinging to it like dew in a meadow.

Yeah, the man knew something, but by the narrow tease of his eyes and the curl of his lips, Kathryn would have better luck deciphering the meaning behind Stonehenge before being allowed into the secret vaults of Paco's mind.

"Fine," she said, not bothering to push it any further. "Can you at least tell me if I have anything to worry about?"

"Worry, no," he said, dismissing her concerns with a subtle shake of the head and a growing smile. "If anyone needs to worry, it's Jake." That comment piqued her interest. "Because you're many things, Kathryn Chase, but patient isn't one of them."

"I can be patient," she said without an iota of conviction.

"Prove it. Let Jake tell you in his own time."

"Since when is patience a punishable offense? Where's the reward?"

"Punishment is your reward," Paco sang, his glee apparent as he summoned the manicurists back over, a clear signal that any chatting about private matters was now done. "Let's get wrapped up here and move on to our massages. Unless, of course, you want me to test your patience on that as well."

Damn this man. Not only could he manipulate her, using her own weaknesses against her, but he always managed to do it with the charisma of the devil and the smile of a saint.

"*Ahh-ha-ha.*" Kathryn giggled as the woman's hands tickled her feet, stripping away her feigned pout. "This is why I never get pedicures."

But the tingling that traveled across her foot was worth it as the rest of her toes would now be the pretty pink piggies they deserved.

"You're ticklish." Paco grinned her way. "I'll bet Jake has a lot of fun with that little tidbit."

And he did, in so many ways that rocked Kathryn from the top of her head to the tips of her toes. But it was her turn to enjoy a long sip and say nothing more than *hmm*.

5

JAKE

"What do you think?" Jake asked the only person he'd trust to help him on a mission like this. His confidant. A true vault.

"It's hard to say," Paco said honestly, which made Jake feel better.

Paco made multibillion-dollar decisions day in and day out, and he made them look damned easy. Clearly, this decision was harder than it looked.

"Let's see that one." With two pristinely manicured fingers, Paco caught the salesman's attention and pointed to the item he had in mind.

Imagining Kathryn's nails would look just as polished, though a shade pinker and to her liking, Jake asked, "How was spa day?"

"A total bust," Paco said with breathy disappointment. "She knows where you were."

"You told her?"

"I didn't have to. She's a kick-ass investigator, and you roped me into an atrocious attempt at deception. I had to come up with spa day on the fly. Oh, and word to the wise—phone finders work both ways."

Jake rubbed his scruffy chin. "My little investigator tracked me back."

"Well, you must be acting suspicious as hell. Extended trips 'out of town,'" Paco said with air quotes. "Turning up at a club? You two share a connection. And curiosity about the lifestyle is sure to be on her mind."

The salesclerk presented the delicate piece of fine jewelry. "Twenty carats of diamonds set in eighteen-karat gold. We can customize it any way you like," he said before stepping away to give them some privacy.

Granted, money was no object. And it wasn't gawdy in any respect. It was breathtaking.

The piece of jewelry was missing something, though. But what? What would make it say *Kathryn*?

Paco snapped it up and stepped over to the full-length mirror, fondling the sparkly masterpiece under the light before holding it against the skin of his neck just above his shirt. Chin high, he admired his reflection like the Armani-clad Miss America he was.

Gruffly, Jake cleared his throat. "You act as if I'm buying it for you."

"You're not? But it goes perfectly with my eyes." Paco batted his eyes adoringly, quickly earning him an eye roll in return.

A small vibration hummed from Jake's watch. An incoming alert. Squinting to read the miniscule print, he resolved to swallow his pride and order those reading glasses already.

Welcome, Master Jake
Check-in: 7:55 p.m.

He glared at the screen, undecided how to tackle this properly. With kid gloves, or a cat-o'-nine-tails? Despite Paco's intense preoccupation with preening, Jake knew better.

"You can't pretend with me, man. I know you read it."

"And I have so many theories. But from the vein throbbing in your temple and who knows where else, this little shopping spree will have to wait."

"Nope. Two birds, one stone."

Paco sighed as he set down the mirror. "Okay, just to be clear, I don't know who came up with that saying, but it's seriously twisted."

"Here." Jake handed his black card to the salesclerk eager to accept it. "I'll take it. I need it gift wrapped."

"Thank you, sir."

He glanced at the clerk's nametag. "Anthony, I'm in a bit of a rush."

"Of course, sir. Be right back." Anthony snapped up the card and left to complete the transaction.

"And, uh, Paco—"

"I've got you. I'll head to your place and put it in your safe."

Jake shook his head in amazement. "I've come to terms with you having access to my home because it's technically an alternate headquarters, but how do you have access to my safe? I've never shown you where it is, and it requires a palm print to open."

"Oh, my dear friend." Paco clucked his tongue. "In the event anything happens to you, the contents of that little safe have to be retrieved pronto. It's stamped with the same tattoo I've got on my ass. *D-G-I*. I can access any of our assets. Me and two of my closest friends."

One was Alex Drake himself, the CEO of DGI, and in the loosest context possible, Paco's boss. The other man with an all-access pass was Alex's most competitive rival, and oddly enough, his best friend, Mark Donovan. And Mark was in the most literal sense Jake's boss.

"Just stay out of my underwear drawer."

"Fine. I prefer Kathryn's anyway."

Rushed, Jake scrawled his electronic signature authorizing the expense worth more than a small island, then pocketed his credit card. He'd known battle and had nearly lost his life. Twice. But this—*this* was what caused his pulse to kick up and his palms to sweat?

"Receipt in the bag?" Anthony asked, beaming from ear to ear.

Paco nodded, taking way too much ownership of the extravagant item. As they headed out, he said, "Don't worry. Receipt on your desk. Royal jewels in the safe. After a quick try-on."

Resigned, Jake shook his head. "As long as her underwear drawer is spared."

"No promises."

He and Paco exchanged a quick bro hug before the first wave of doubt settled in.

Worried, he looked Paco in the eye. "No bullshit. Do you think she'll like it?"

Paco placed a reassuring hand on Jake's shoulder, giving it a confident squeeze. "If she doesn't, I'll do you the solid of taking it off your hands." With a bright, beaming grin, Paco patted his arm and sent him on his way. "No buyer's remorse. It's perfect. Now get the fuck out of here, or I really will keep it."

"Thanks," Jake called after him, picking up the pace as he headed out.

After climbing into his F-150 Raptor, Jake started the engine and headed toward the freeway, ready to drive a route he knew by heart, no matter how many years it had been since he was last there.

Jake took an extra-long second rereading Kathryn's last text. "Fuck."

KATHRYN: Girls' night with Julian. Be home late. Love you.

His clever little kitten hadn't lied. Well, not exactly. But it was close enough to earn more than the disappointment of her man. She'd just earned the wrath of her Dom, and with a half-cocked smile, Jake considered the punishment.

Swift, long, and hard. It was time his little kitten learned her boundaries as a sub.

6
KATHRYN

"Jeez, this outfit is tight," Kathryn muttered under her breath. Fidgeting, she tugged the ultra-short skirt of her sexy outfit lower, as far as it would stretch, her futile attempt to keep her coochie from hypothermia.

She took a sharp look around Club Lazarus. The lighting was dim, but not dark, and she could make out the halls beyond the great foyer. The energy was vibrant and electric, intoxicating and mysterious.

But does it have to be so damn cold?

She'd imagined her first time at a BDSM club required a certain look. This was the tightest skirt she owned, and the highest heels. With a lace corset she'd bought on a whim and vowed she'd never wear, her risqué ensemble wasn't half bad, but she cursed herself for not bringing a jacket. The room's temperature rivaled that of a vodka bar, though it probably kept sweat to a minimum. And without a doubt, people came to sweat.

Her date seemed just as reluctant, second-guessing his outfit the whole ride over.

"Tight?" Julian huffed. "Try squeezing into this."

Kathryn stole a daring glance, scanning her best friend's bare and hairless chest, past the six-pack that was the result of his suicide-inducing no-sugar diet, finally down to his package.

Medically speaking, Julian was endowed. Nonmedically, the man was a stallion. A stallion that broke one too many a woman's heart with the mournful news that he was gay.

The pleather ensemble securing his manhood was being stretched well beyond its strength and integrity. The man was a deep breath away from slicing through his pants like butter with the cock he'd aptly named Excalibur. Admittedly, his ass looked smoking hot in it, which made Kathryn half consider trying those ridiculous squats he always yammered on about.

"Trust me," he said. "For person or persons I hook up with tonight, no need to spring for lube. I'm covered," he said, gesturing to his thighs where his pants clung like Saran Wrap.

Horrified, Kathryn let out a gasp. "Your leggings are full of lube?"

"There was no way this look was happening unless Daddy topped off the tank."

"Good luck getting those babies off."

"That, my dear Kathryn, is what my Dom is for."

She slammed her eyes shut. "I weep for your dry cleaner."

"Don't weep too hard. My dry cleaning paid for his Tesla. Morty has no complaints."

"My ten bucks says Morty never gives you a discount, either."

"Look, it was this or a slingshot."

"The term is mankini," Kathryn said, correcting him as she pantomimed a *V* from his shoulders to his crotch.

Julian scoffed. "The term is *painful*. You take a speedo, and stretch the band halfway to Canada getting it up and over your shoulders. Trust me, these might as well be my buffet pants for how comfy they are compared to a pair of those." He propped his hands on his hips and looked around the club's exquisite lobby where they waited. "Tell me again why you wanted me here and not Jake."

Yeah. She'd been a little vague. Intentionally so.

Kathryn shrugged, focusing her attention on tugging up her strapless corset. Her boobs were a quarter inch away from popping out. "I just wanted to check it out."

Yes, she'd just wanted to check out a lifestyle club way across town. To see what she was in for. And with Jake taking his sweet time bringing her, she couldn't help the increasing number of questions she had about it. And it was the one club he hadn't been to, based on the snooping she'd done with their phone-finder app, so the chance of running into him here was nil.

"It's no big deal," she said to Julian. "I just want to see what I'm in for."

Tired of waiting, she took a few determined steps toward the unmanned reception desk and scanned the back room for the attendant. Or bouncer. Or whoever might give them entry. Normally, she'd bypass all this gatekeeper bullshit, but this was a house of BDSM, and punishment, no doubt, would be swift.

"Wait. You mean for the first time?" Julian took a cautious step back as his eyes grew alarmingly wide. "Without Jake? Are you telling me Jake doesn't know you're here? *We're* here?"

Meekly, she shook her head, swallowing the guilt of misleading both Julian and Jake.

"Wow. You really have no idea how this Dom/sub thing works. Coming to a club without your Dom? You won't be able to sit for a week."

"It'll be fine. I'll just explain."

With a wary scoff, Julian cupped her cheek. "That'll sort of be hard with a ball gag lodged in your mouth."

Before Kathryn could give several very logical and reasonable explanations for why she'd venture to a club without her Dom, the man she would marry, a woman hurried to the front desk to greet them.

"Sorry for your wait. Someone called out sick. I'm—"

"Andi," Kathryn said, the name lodging in her throat. Her student had completely transformed, with her black pixie cut slicked back, and her breasts a sigh away from spilling out of a bright red corset dress, her dark eyes pinned Kathryn's.

Andi's spark of recognition was instant, brightening her face with a friendly smile. "Right, Kathryn. Or is it Kat?" Andi leaned in, her tone reassuring as she said, "It's all right. What happens here, stays here. Locked up like Vegas."

Kill me now.

"Actually," Julian said, "tonight, let's call her Lolita."

Considering the options, Kathryn played along. After all, this was a place to shed your inhibitions with the occasional alias.

Standing taller and pushing out her girls proudly, Kathryn accepted her stage name. For the next hour or so, she would be Lolita. Daring with a naughty side that said *anything goes*.

In truth, nothing would be going. It would be like strolling through Jared's. Just browsing. No payment plans. Not buying.

I am, after all, engaged.

Andi took several exaggerated pecks at the keyboard. "Lo-li-ta," she said, sounding out the name for effect before giving Kathryn a wink. "And who's your friend, Lolita?"

With a few brisk pats on Julian's back, Kathryn said, "This is . . . Bucky." The laugh she nearly snorted out was instantly quieted by Julian's scowl.

But before he could object, Andi hit those five little keys.

"B-u-c-k-y." She pecked in his alias, then return her smile to them both. "Great. Lolita and Bucky." Tilting her head, Andi sized up the two of them before locking her gaze with Kathryn's. "Does your sub need a preference sheet?"

Why am I the Dom?

Giddy, Julian patted her shoulder. "Fear not, little girl. Someday you'll be a real sub."

"Perhaps I should have worn my pleather leggings. Too bad I forgot to pick up my gallon of lube." Redirecting her attention to Andi, Kathryn said, "I'm a sub too. And no need for his preference sheet. Bucky here hands them out like business cards."

"Speaking of business cards," Andi said, frowning as she lightly bit her lower lip and scanned the computer screen. "I don't see either of your names in the system as members, and unless you've been vouched for by a member and vetted, you can't enter. I'd like to help, but I don't know you well enough to let you in." Andi glanced away, avoiding a confrontation.

"Oh, didn't I give you the name up front?" Julian said. "Jake Russo."

As Andi looked it up, Kathryn tossed him an annoyed glare.

"Ah, yes. Of course. Mr. Russo—I mean, Bucky. And thank you for your membership. Is there anything I can get either of you before you enter?"

She gestured to the wall of erotic paraphernalia behind her, including clamps, plugs, and every type of dildo known to man, woman, and in the infinite words of *Kinky Boots*, "those who have yet to decide." A glossy whip drew Kathryn's interest for half a second before she noticed various types of bondage gear. Especially the ropes.

"We have a membership sale going on. Twenty-percent off everything."

"Ooh, a sale. Am I able to charge it to my account?" Julian asked enthusiastically. Kathryn gave his arm a chastising smack.

Julian grinned. "And you wonder why people think you're a Dom."

"Yes. And we have more exclusive items in our high-end room, if you need to take a look," Andi said, but both Kathryn and Julian shook their heads, polite as they declined. "His and hers locker rooms are down the hall. Towels and water are in every room. *Red* is the recognized safe word by all Dungeon Masters. If you prefer another one, please notify them. And we recommend you stay out of the Abyss unless you know what you're doing."

"I'd seriously kill for your cocktail list," Kathryn said hopefully as she licked her lips, and was surprised by Julian's jab to her ribs. Glaring at him, she huffed out, "*Ow.*"

Julian barked out a laugh. His fake laugh. With that, along with his actor's smile and stern brows, she got it. Julian's warning was clear. She was far from Kansas, and asking for a drink was committing some bizarre club faux pas.

I just want to take the edge off. How wrong can it be?

"Honey," he said in a scolding tone. "You know there's no alcohol in here."

What the hell?

"Right. There's not." Kathryn leaned close to his ear. "It's BYOB?"

"It's a place where everyone holds tight to their faculties. At all times," he said low through clenched teeth. "Actually . . ." He turned his attention back to Andi, reigniting his winning smile. "Dirty Lolita could use her own preference sheet. And a pen."

Andi handed a clear clipboard to Kathryn with a sheet of paper and a bright red pen. "It's double-sided," she said, pointing helpfully to the sheet.

"Oh, I don't . . ." Kathryn paused before handing it back. Along the left-hand side was a laundry list of possibilities, though it was customized a little differently than the one Jake had given her.

The dizzying list of restraints and gags alone boggled her mind. When she reviewed five different types of gags, she instinctively blurted, "I'm allergic to adhesive."

Both Andi and Julian stared and blinked.

Tapping the sheet with his finger, Julian pointed to the box she should mark. "Hard limit, honey."

"You can take that with you," Andi said. "Maybe work through it as you move into various areas of play. Need me to show you around?"

"No. We're good. Thanks." Julian hooked an arm through Kathryn's, leading her away while humming the tune to "We're Off to See the Wizard."

The man needs help.

7

KATHRYN

With her arm linked with Julian's, Kathryn enjoyed a leisurely stroll through Club Lazarus. The evenly staggered low-voltage sconces along the hall gave her just enough light to read the preference sheet, but barely.

Squinting, she asked, "What's the difference between a small anal plug and a large one?"

Julian's comfortable pace came to an abrupt halt. "It's sort of subjective."

He moved his hands from close together to outrageously far apart, demonstrating for Kathryn's benefit that the sizes could range from a little over an inch to roughly the size of a rocket launcher.

She rolled her eyes. "You're saying getting something shoved up your ass could be a choking hazard?"

Shrugging, he grinned with delight.

"What's the biggest you've, ahem, seen?"

"Mind you, I've never partaken of the Wildebeest, but I'd compare it to three cans of soda stacked one on top of the other."

Kathryn smacked a hand to her mouth, realizing every word of Julian's study of the wild had to be true. The thought made her gasp. And clench.

"Perhaps you should fill that out with Jake. Hint-hint." Julian's patience was waning. "Just tell me why he's not here. And don't say he's out of town, because I know he isn't."

"Wait. How do you know that?"

"Nope. Not until you spill. Here."

Julian gripped her elbow, leading her to a cushioned bench. There seemed to be a lot of them around the place. Some with joysticks. Kathryn took a seat, squinting and realizing *that's not a joystick*.

Scooting a few inches to the side, she set down the clipboard and clasped her hands, preparing for a lecture from her semi-nude professor. But in her fantasies, her semi-nude professor was straight and had her strapped to his desk.

Ready for a nonsexual tongue-lashing, she looked up at him sweetly. "What do you want to know, Master Bucky?"

"Start with why you and I are here. And why you seem to know less about BDSM than the sisters of Saint Francis."

"I just . . ." Her shoulders dropped. "I don't want Jake to be disappointed. This would be the next logical step in our relationship and . . . it's no big deal. I'm doing what I always do. Research. I don't want to look like I don't have a clue."

Julian cupped her cheeks in his incredibly soft hands. "I love how you think he doesn't know."

Helplessly, she sighed. "Maybe you're right. We should go."

"After I've exhausted my entire supply of lube? Not on your life. I can't even begin to tell you what it took for me to get you in here. Sure, your rushed health screening was just the start. And I haven't been a member long enough to vouch for you, so I improvised. Which means, my little sub, we're staying, and I'm happy to be your seeing-eye Dom for this leg of your tour."

Jumping to her feet, Kathryn stood on tiptoe to hug his neck, squealing as she thanked him profusely.

Julian gave her a reassuring squeeze. "Anytime. Come on. Let's explore this kinky little underworld you'll soon be calling home."

"Not yet. How did you know Jake wasn't out of town?"

Giving her a grin, Julian lowered his voice. "Because he called me earlier, very much in town. He needed some advice."

"On what?" Kathryn asked, taking his arm to resume their slow stroll.

"Same thing as you," he teased. "Research."

Kathryn's next question was interrupted by noises from a nearby room. The loud moans caught her off guard, the sweet and tortured sounds of pleasure stopping her in her tracks.

"Want to peek inside?" Julian asked, pointing to a door that was left slightly ajar.

"No," she said firmly, then whispered, "Let's just give them their privacy."

"Rule number one," Julian said, clearly enjoying his teaching moment. "When a door is left open, you're free to look. Wide open, and it's actually preferred."

"What?"

Frozen in place and only half considering it, Kathryn couldn't bring herself to move toward the open door—the one beckoning with the sounds of want and lust. And sex. A lot of sex.

She'd never seen other people having sex. Not real sex. Not even porn. And sex on a soap opera hardly qualified.

"I don't think I can," she whispered.

"Well, you're smack dab in the middle of a sex club. You're dirty Dorothy Gale, and I'm your hard Tin Man. Trust me, when we find the curtain the Wizard is hiding behind, he'll be fucking. Besides, you're a nurse. You've seen naked people."

"Naked, yes. Fucking, no."

"Think of it as medical research and not salacious gawking."

His double-dare glare was all she needed to peek inside.

Sure enough, a burly man was plowing into the backside of a woman who was blindfolded and strapped to a bench. Like the bench Kathryn had sat on not five minutes ago.

Ugh, I need a shower.

Yet, she stayed, *researching* wide-eyed as two total strangers went at it. With his strong fingers woven through the woman's hair, the man shoved more of his length in, plowing into her in a steady rhythm that said just one thing. Control.

Kathryn's breathing shallowed, taking on a rhythm—their rhythm. Her body temperate shot up as her core clenched. It was the first time she'd actually seen sex. Watched it. Studied how a man took a woman. And it was hot.

The man looked up, locking eyes with Kathryn. And like a professional nurse—or an unwavering voyeur—she stared back, unable to turn away.

The amused smile on his face said just one thing. He enjoyed this. Being in the spotlight. Having an audience.

Is he putting on a show?

He smacked his hand briskly on the woman's ass, and she moaned. After one last thrust, he ended it. Without satisfying either of them, he pulled out.

"We have company," he said low to the woman still strapped to the bench. "Let's show her how you take me down your throat."

Two taps on her shoulder startled Kathryn.

"Ready?" Julian asked, as if she might have been window-shopping for a pair of shoes instead of losing herself in raw, untamed voyeurism. "Or should I grab you some popcorn?"

"*Mm-hmm.*" Forming words wasn't an option, and the subarctic temperature didn't prevent a bead of sweat from making its way down her back.

Kathryn fanned her face as they made their way farther down the hall, reminding herself over and over again that this was research. Pure, scientific, Masters and Johnson meets whips and chains *research.*

Sure, having Jake with her was preferred. With another glance at Julian's freshly waxed chest, she mentally reinforced those words.

Definitely. Preferred.

Would Jake be upset, having missed out on her first steps over the threshold into a world that was more his than hers?

Jake couldn't be mad. She and Julian just happened upon this club.

Happened upon it forty minutes outside the city on a "girls' night." And it might have been a little off the beaten path . . . with some insane directions Julian knew by heart. His step-by-step directions as she drove led them down a moderately winding but very dark road. They nearly hit two separate deer, and because Julian had actually been there a time or ten, his *turn at the next dirt road* callouts were the only way they ever got there. In hindsight, she probably should have left behind some bread crumbs. Just in case.

Julian was one of her best friends and a definite girls' girl. It takes a special kind of friend to hear, "I need to bust into a sex club and check it out," and immediately respond with, "What should I wear?"

Still amazed, she scanned his wardrobe selection. To clarify, all she'd said was *you can't go wrong with black*. Finding pants that were tighter than a condom and screamed *peel my banana with your teeth* were all on him.

"How do you know so much about clubs?" she asked under her breath.

"You're engaged to an infamous Dom. How do you not?"

Infamous? Infamous. As in being famous for his bad, bad deeds. As a Dom. *Infamous* didn't happen within the privacy of his home. And *infamous* didn't happen with just one person.

Did it?

There was a hunger in Kathryn. A need. A yearning to explore that careful blend of pleasure and pain. Succumbing to submission. To desires. To him. Her gaze dropped to the ring on her finger.

"Shit." Kathryn huffed, looking at the sparkling engagement ring on her hand. "I forgot to leave this at home."

"Don't worry. Lots of couples here are married. And if anyone asks, I'm your spouse."

"True enough," she said, nodding in agreement.

Julian glanced at her neck, frowning as regret flashed across his face. "We probably should have gotten you a collar."

Checking her outfit, she took the fashionista biker's critique with a grain of salt. Seriously, she was an ostrich feather short of being a can-can girl. "I'm not sure adding to this outfit is the answer."

Deadpan, Julian gave her several slow blinks of disbelief. "You're kidding."

"What?" Kathryn might have recalled random mentions of a collar here and there. Faking her adamance, she raised her hand between them, giving Julian an up-close look at the ring with a stone that a Kardashian would have envied. "This is all the collar I need."

"Not in here."

Frowning, she asked, "Why not?"

Julian's forehead dropped into the palm of his hand, giving Kathryn a better understanding of how little, in fact, she did know. "Oh my God. No, child. A collar means you're owned. Otherwise, you're sort of fair game."

In an instant, the subarctic temperature thawed as heat swept up her arms, neck, and face.

Self-consciously touching her bare neck, she gasped. "Really?"

Julian's hand landed firmly on her shoulder. "Don't worry. I'm sure they've got one at the front desk." In a show of solidarity and with enough sass to strike a nerve, he selflessly volunteered. "It's all right. Remember, in the role of Jake Russo and for one night only, I'll be your Dom."

Glaring at him, Kathryn crossed her arms over her chest. "Don't forget. Andi thought I was *your* Dom."

"Yes, and if only there were more like Andi to go around," he said with a snicker. "All I want is a little time on a Saint Andrews cross at the hand of a hot daddy until I'm begging for the mercy of his rock-solid stick."

Kathryn shook her head with a little shudder. "I did not need that visual."

Ignoring her, he continued. "But look at me." Julian stood, all six-foot-one of him, proud to showcase a hundred eighty-five pounds of lean, mean gay sex-god machine. "No matter how I try to downplay it, this pretty package of heavenly goodness screams Dom all night long."

Giving a few playful squeezes to the bulging muscles of his arm, Kathryn smiled. "Maybe you should let yourself go a little. Eat something other than salad."

"I think we both know I'm too vain for that."

"True," she said, ready to move on.

Looking up and down the dim corridor, she couldn't be certain which way they had come. And by the indecision on Julian's face, maybe he couldn't either.

"Remind me again why you refused the escort?"

"I know how to get to the lobby. It's just a ways back. But you'll be alone . . . unless you want to come with me."

"I'm fine," she lied. "Besides, if you stick around too long with me, every hot Dom in the place will think you're straight."

With a paternal hand on her shoulder and dipping his head down enough to be nearly eye-to-eye, he said, "They haven't for the last ten years." Julian planted a consoling kiss to her forehead. "Don't stray too far. I'll be right back with a collar for you."

Breezing past them, a tall man with tattooed shoulders, a delectable eight-pack, and a magnetic smile gave them a wink before deliberately squeezing between them, wearing just the type of mankini they'd quarreled over. Proud as a bungee-wrapped peacock, he sported his impressive package in the tiniest wrapper known to man.

Both Kathryn and Julian turned, following the man with their wide-eyed stares. The exposed taut muscles of his ass munching on the backside of the slingshot proved Kathryn's point.

"*That* does not look comfortable," she murmured.

Julian hummed under his breath. "True. Delicious and lickable, but definitely not comfortable. Perhaps I should recommend he take it off."

"Hey, you're supposed to be on a mission for my collar."

"Can I help it if that scrumptious ass happens to be going the same way I'm heading? Wait here and finish your preference sheet. If you need help, just say *red*. Any Dungeon Master will help."

"Dungeon Master?"

"Think of them as wardens. Their word is law. But they're also first responders. They make sure everyone is playing by the rules and no one gets hurt. They can be any gender. In Club Lazarus, they're the ones in the masks."

Julian hurried down the hall and vanished around the corner, chasing the man with the lickable ass. With her luck, Kathryn would be getting collared four or five hours from now.

8

KATHRYN

Fifteen minutes into her wait, Kathryn was itching to move. She needed some frame of reference to fill out the sheet, and other than spanking and edging, she might as well have been a virgin.

Kathryn continued exploring, meandering down one dark passage after another. At least down this hall there were a few open rooms she could glance into. And for the doors that weren't open, she had to at least listen. Obviously, behind those doors had to be where the true kink reared its naughty head.

In the first room she paused at, a woman was standing over a man who lay motionless on the floor before her.

Kathryn needed to rein in her nursing instincts. He wasn't hurt. At least, he wasn't the sort of hurt that required medical attention. He just lay still on the questionably clean floor wearing a scrap of cloth that made Speedos look like boxers.

The woman, obviously his Dominatrix, placed her stiletto heel gently on his bare chest before digging it in a little and hitting his sternum. "Did I say you could move?" she snapped sharply.

The man let out a guttural, sensual moan. "No, Mistress."

The scene wasn't grabbing Kathryn's attention as much as the man was. Or rather, his neck. He had a collar.

She studied the simple leather strap laden with silver spikes and a small ring at the front. It was easy to imagine a leash tethered to it. As easy as it was to imagine a similar collar snug around her own neck. Was Jake the sort of Dom to use one? A leash?

I've been with this man for months. I've memorized every scar. Know his tattoos like the back of my hand. How do I not know these things? Like, I don't know him at all.

The more she thought about it, the more she wanted to know him. All of him. Chisel away the protective layers that held in his molten heat. Discover the real Jake Russo, one kink at a time.

With her hand softly caressing the naked skin on her neck, Kathryn was just now catching on that the door wasn't open. There was no door. At all. This small room was a stage. And an opportunity she had to explore.

Determined with her preference sheet front and center, she watched with intention, gauging her level of interest by the sensations of her nether regions. Heat equaled interest.

The Dominatrix began by berating every part of him, from his selection of attire to the nearly invisible size of his dick which, even from as far away as Kathryn stood, couldn't be further from the truth.

Humiliation. Ice cold.

"Stroke yourself," she said. "That's it."

Forced orders. Forced pleasure. Definitely warmer. Check and check.

"Don't come." The command was dark and low, dripping with power. Two little words that made a Dom a Dom, and a sub a sub. Two words Kathryn had heard so many times before.

Kathryn's thighs clenched together. That thought stirred a small fire. When the Dominatrix added, "Not until I tell you to," in an instant, she was wet. Panting, her nipples peaked hard beneath the tight fabric of her bustier, and all she wanted was Jake.

"On your hands and knees," the Dominatrix commanded.

This is getting good.

The man snapped into place, practically whimpering as he took his stance on all fours. With her hand on his cheek, she gave him a tender caress and moved toward his ear but didn't lower her voice.

"Someone is watching you," she said, her dark eyes on Kathryn, and turned his face so he looked as well.

Mortified but too embarrassed to move away, Kathryn froze, meeting the woman's gaze.

With a warm smile, she invited Kathryn to the intimacy of their scene. "Come in and watch if you like."

"No, thank you," she said, in a meek voice that barely made it past her lips.

The Dominatrix only nodded and smiled, understanding and not imposing at all. Relieved, Kathryn smiled her appreciation as the Dom refocused her attention to her sub.

It was then that Kathryn noticed the wall behind the couple in play. It was hung with an assortment of small and large whips, gags, dildos of an imaginative range of styles and sizes, and as luck would have it, a collar. A rather plain one not nearly half as interesting as the one the man wore, but it would do.

As the Dominatrix circled her prey, Kathryn couldn't possibly interrupt. She checked her watch.

How long does this last?

"On your back," the woman said more harshly than before, and Kathryn noticed a small smile forming on the man's lips.

Attentive to each movement, she watched the scene unfold.

The Dominatrix swung her leg across the man, intentionally but lightly slicing his skin with the sharp edge of her heel. With her feet placed on each side of him, she inched her skirt higher. Lowering herself, she hovered in a squat but refrained from touching him.

Kathryn had wanted research, and this was research. Just two lab rats going at it while she took notes.

"Please, Mistress," the man said. "Please."

On cue, the Dominatrix gave her sub exactly what he wanted. And gave it to him about half a second too late before Kathryn could slam her eyes shut. She'd heard of it. The act was referred to as a golden shower and definitely warranted a door, if for no other reason than to provide the random passerby a splatter guard.

Promptly moving on, she pressed the red pen hard to the *No* column of the preference sheet.

Unless I'm trapped at the bottom of a cavern for three days, urine, for any other reason, is out. Whoever's doing the cleanup in aisle five should be sainted.

Safe from catching a whiff of ammonia, Kathryn thanked her lucky stars that the next door she encountered was closed. Cautiously, she pressed her ear against it, easily recognizing there were several participants carrying on their own private scene.

Smack. Smack. Groan.

Kathryn's core throbbed. Julian was right. She shouldn't be here without Jake.

Reaching for her phone, she sighed, remembering she had no pockets. Her phone was in the car.

Okay, so she had no way to call Julian, though considering he'd left his phone with her car keys in a locker, calling him would do no good. Even if she shouted his name at the top of her lungs, which she was more than half tempted to do, this wasn't exactly the sort of place where anyone would bat an eye. They'd just assume another sub was taking it good for her Master.

She'd long stopped leering in each passing room, moving swiftly in the hope of finding Julian and heading home. But the place was much bigger than it looked. Her Army training meant she could find her way guided by nothing more than the moon and the stars. But without the sky as a reference, the trail of moans, slaps, and tickles seemed to be getting her nowhere. Fast.

At the end of the next hall, she decided to make a left at the T, turning down a particularly dark passage. With its walls painted black, the ambience here was decidedly more sinister. If there were any more doors down this short hall, she couldn't see them. Her pulse kicked up a notch.

Having turned another corner, Kathryn was startled to come face-to-face with a masked man. The hall wasn't exactly narrow, but the hard, chiseled lines of his granite body easily filled the space.

Perhaps he was a Dungeon Master. Warden. First responder. And in his skintight leather outfit and his face covered, he was lust incarnate—the Devil himself if the devil was masked. Asking him for directions out of here would be smart, but the muscular god pinned her with a stare that stole her breath.

Keeping a small distance between them, he said nothing, letting the slow, predatory movements of his body speak volumes in the shadows and darkness. And, *damn*, if he didn't have plenty to say. His body was perfect. Kathryn could only stand there, stunned and still.

The leather mask covered only the top half of his face, but it was enough to send shock waves to her core. His full lips simmered just below a smile, and his stare made a lazy path down her body and up again. Like she was utterly naked. Wanting and naked.

Maybe it was the pheromones. This place had to be an atom bomb of hormones.

Should I be taking notes?

Kathryn let her libido indulge itself, shifting her gaze freely past the tight leather vest with nothing underneath to the sensual muscles of his shadowy neck, shoulders, and arms. The man was glorious. He was pure sex and seduction, danger and sin, all wrapped up in a skintight outfit that was designed to emphasize one big thing. His package.

And when I say his package, I mean his cock. The damn thing is huge.

His leather pants were laced at the crotch, a personal Christmas gift she wanted to open. With her teeth. And laced up so thankfully tight, the anaconda wouldn't be able to penetrate her from the several feet they stood apart. She hoped.

Every inch of him was sexy. *He* was sexy.

Was this why Jake kept her from these clubs? Her fiancé had made it clear he didn't like to share. In his infinite wisdom, he knew. Knew that her rational thought would shut down like a freeway at rush hour. Knew that attraction was primal. In a sexually charged situation like this, her cave-girl instincts would naturally kick in, spiking her pulse, tightening her nipples, and filling her core with the pressure of Mount Vesuvius minutes before the eruption.

Gridlocked in a stalemate of awkward, lust-filled silence, Kathryn remained fixed under his gaze. Blinking, breathing, and not doing much else, she made a small gesture to try to snap out of it, managing to nip at her lower lip.

In no uncertain terms, this guy was a living, breathing billboard screaming ENTER IF YOU DARE.

No, no, no, no, nooo. I do not dare.

But from a purely clinical perspective, there was no denying the strange response of her body. The match strike to her core. The bonfire of heat. The way every cell of her body stood at attention, anticipating even the slightest go-signal from her bossy, overcharged lizard brain.

Her reaction was sexual attraction at its most raw, unsophisticated, carnal form. Fascinating in the classroom. Inconvenient at the moment. Its intensity robbed her of even her most basic abilities, like stepping away. And breathing.

What am I, nineteen? Just turn around, put one foot in front of the other, and walk away.

Before she could do exactly that, the Dungeon Master took a bold step closer.

Or . . . I can invest in a chastity belt.

Instead of giving her space or shying away from her curiosity, he seemed to relish it, again moving his own hungry gaze up and down her body in kind. And invitation. Which instantly raised the blush level of her cheeks to red-hot as he took one more step.

Insistent and in an embarrassingly loud voice, she blurted, "I'm not having sex with you!"

Even from beneath his foreboding mask, nothing could hide the amused pop of his brow. Her commanding, heartfelt words did nothing but fall on deaf ears. He closed in, making another dangerous move in her direction.

Lizard brain aside, Kathryn had just enough presence of mind to back away, an evasive tactic that unfortunately managed to pin her against a wall. He propped his hands on the wall on either side of her, caging her in.

"Hey," she said, breathy in forced protest.

He only grinned.

Stunned at his forwardness, she shifted her weight, readying her knee for a sharp strike. But this close, the strange glow in the darkness gave his features character, just enough to catch all of his brashness. His arrogance. His persistence. A dominance that materialized in faint familiarity and a dirty little half smile.

"Well, hello, Daddy," Julian said, finally returning from his trek to Antarctica, unbothered that his best friend was two seconds away from a cavity search by this man's cock.

Instead, her bestie waved the collar he'd gone in search of, and playfully ran his free hand flirtatiously along the man's arm.

Still holding Kathryn's gaze, the Dungeon Master simply said, "Hey, Julian."

9

KATHRYN

"Jake?"

Before Kathryn could squeak out another word, Jake flung her over his shoulder like a tawdry burlesque-dressed sack of potatoes. Any hope for protest, or explanation, was impossible. Her time at Club Lazarus seemed to be over.

"How about a little help?" she begged Julian.

"I've got a better idea," Jake said to his number one fan. "You and Kathryn came here in the Maserati? Keep it."

"Really?" Julian the traitor said with delight.

"Yup. For the next week. Locker number and combination, kitten. I assume that's where you left the car keys."

Jake wasn't asking. It was a demand. Her delayed response resulted in a terse swat on her left ass cheek.

"Okay, okay," she said with a giggle. "Locker number seven. The combo is four-three-two-one."

Jake's entire body stiffened, freezing at the ridiculously over simplified code. "Have I taught you nothing?"

"Apparently so," Julian said, handing him the collar. "Later."

As Julian scurried away, Jake took a deep sigh and stomped in the other direction.

"Jake," she choked out upside down, not pausing his determined stride one little bit.

It was another voice that stopped him. An unnerving voice that Kathryn recognized.

"Jake?" the sugary voice called after him.

"Shit," he muttered under his breath.

"Is that you?"

At the sound of that singsong voice, Jake turned around in a perfect military about-face as Kathryn's mind spun.

That voice. I know that voice. God, tell me that's not—

"Hey, Chels," Jake said, shifting Kathryn on his shoulder so her short-skirted ass was now in a peek-a-boo stare-down with his ex-fiancée's face.

Kathryn noted that in the midst of everything, Chelsea Anders, the woman desperate to be known as Chelsea Russo, happened to recognize Jake easily despite his mask. Instinctually. Annoyingly.

If my nips and vagina can pick him out of a lineup, that counts. Right?

"Wow, you look amazing," Chelsea gushed, cozying up so close to Kathryn's fiancé, if she were any closer, she'd be licking Kathryn's butt instead of kissing Jake's.

Yes, Jake. You look amazing. Now put me down. How about a proper introduction? As. Your. Fiancée.

"Thanks," he had the audacity to say. Brazenly, he followed it up with, "So do you."

Great. I'm jealous, pissed off, and now all I can wonder is what she's wearing. And if she looks better than me. I've been downgraded from nineteen-year-old to flat-out middle schooler. What the hell?

Kathryn struggled to be set down, which did nothing but earn her another terse smack. This time on the right ass cheek. The mild yelp that left her lips melted to a smile as Jake's warm hand soothed and massaged the cheek he'd barely punished. Right in Chelsea's flawless face.

"Look, Chels, I can't chat. This one's a little antsy for my attention."

Between the deep baritone of his voice that rumbled through her body, and his large, soothing hand resting on her butt, the man wasn't wrong.

He turned and took two steps for the door before Chelsea hustled ahead of him, blocking his path.

"Can I . . . join?"

Appalled, Kathryn stiffened. *No, she can't join!*

"No. You can't join," he said, chuckling when this was no laughing matter.

So many questions. Gee, Jake, why would Chelsea Anders think she could join? Is that what you two used to do? Threesomes? Foursomes? More-somes? No judgment.

Even in the private recesses of Kathryn's mind, it sounded like judgment. But it wasn't.

Hesitation? For sure. Uncertainty? Yes, because isn't that what a sex club is about? Pushing boundaries? Blurring the lines of commitment like the fog smoking off the San Francisco Bay?

Had the idea of two men at the same time ever crossed her mind? Technically, yes.

But in my defense, I'd only imagined it with Jake, and a very different version of Jake—the evil one you can tell by the goatee. But Jake with me and another woman? Another woman who isn't me? Who happened to also have a history with him, including his last name? I might not judge, but consider it one hell of a hard damned limit. Where's my preference sheet?

"Good-bye, Chels," Jake said, the gravity of his tone unmistakable. Decisive. Final.

"Okay." Chelsea sighed with a whimper of regret. "See you around."

"See you around," Kathryn mocked under her breath once they were through the main doors and safely out of earshot.

Her snarkiness earned her one last playful smack on the ass and the gruff order, "Not now."

10

KATHRYN

*J*ake's swift steps took on an agitated roughness, giving Kathryn the sudden realization he wasn't teasing. He was heated, and not in the fun way.

He walked them around to the side of the building, where he lifted his mask before setting her down. "Kathryn, you said you were having girl time with Julian."

"I was." Her technically true comeback was met with the challenge of Jake's scowl. He crossed his arms, and she crossed hers. "And you said you were out of town."

It was just the ammo she needed to unclench his jaw and unknot his arms.

"Truce?" she said, deliberate in pressing herself against him, but his arms didn't wrap around her like they usually did.

Hands planted on his hips, Jake looked down at her with darkening eyes. The natural deepness to his voice became serious and low. "Why come here? Without me?"

His questions were short and direct, like two tiny daggers to the heart. The second she tried to look away, his strong hands cradled her face.

"I don't give a damn about the secrets you keep, but not about this. I own your desires. It's what makes you mine," he said softly, pressing his forehead to hers. "Talk to me, kitten."

Kathryn sucked in a breath, then let the air stagger out. "Because you're an infamous Dom, and I'm *that* girl. The newbie."

"Normally, I'm not a fan of labels, but infamous?" He drew out the word for effect. "You only get to be *new* once. It's important that you experience it right."

"I was just doing—"

"If you say research, you're getting punished." His thumb brushed her full lower lip.

Defiantly, she whispered, "Research," then swallowed. "Why have you been going to sex clubs without me?"

Jake's smile was boyish and coy. "Your luscious butt just ran into one of the reasons."

"Your ex-fiancée?"

He shook his head. "Chels is a very active part of this community and has a lot of friends in it. She can be calculating, jealous, petty—"

"And might still have more than a fleeting infatuation with you?"

His lips firmed into a tight line. "She's a legitimate member who's done nothing wrong. I can't have her blocked. But I can find out which clubs she frequents, which is part of what I've been doing."

"Why not just . . ." Kathryn's voice lowered. "Hack them?"

Jake chuckled, and Kathryn relaxed as his strong arms surrounded her, holding her tight against his chest. "Smart clubs keep their membership off the grid. Impervious to hacking."

"So, no clubs for us?" she asked. It was a blow but a small one. She couldn't miss what she'd never had.

"We could head to clubs out of state, though that might get, well, inconvenient when the urge strikes. So, I've got something else in the works."

"A secret?"

"Let's call it a surprise," he said, and when Kathryn let out an overexcited squeal, he instantly snuffed it out. "But a surprise that will have to wait."

Kathryn's face fell into a pout. "Booo."

"Now . . ." He stood taller. "For the crimes of deceiving your fiancé, entering Club Lazarus without your Dom, and daring to call it research, it's time you learn a little about this world, kitten. And what it means to be punished."

Maybe it was the way he said the word *punished*. Dark. Threatening.

Or the way his fingers walked their way through her hair, enough to get a thick fistful and yank.

Or the way his hard cock pressed eagerly against her belly.

God, I want to be punished.

"Let's see," he said, removing a folded sheet of paper from his back pocket.

Getting a closer look at the skintight pants she'd never seen before, all Kathryn could think is *Are we out of lube too?*

Jake began to mutter. "No to humiliation and urination. Yes to public sex . . ."

Holy hell.

"Where did you get that?" Feebly, she swiped at the page, but Jake lifted it high above her head. She made several jumps to grab it, but it was no use. The man was a giant.

"Your first sex at a sex club, but not *in* a sex club. *Hmm.*" Jake mused aloud, seeming to work out whether this was too much punishment, or not enough. Returning the sheet to his tight back pocket, he donned a wicked grin. "Acceptable."

Kathryn's eyes rounded. "Here? Outside?"

Sex in the isolation of a hot springs late at night is one thing. But here where everyone passing by would see?

"Right here. Right now. And this being your first real punishment, I intend to take my time."

Jake's features hardened, giving his rugged good looks an edge of darkness. His hazel eyes steeled, turning them sinister. Challenging. Forbidden. His cold stare was a warning and a promise all at once, and her heart thundered in the heat of what could only be described as a Dom's gaze.

"You like the mask?" he said, phrasing his question as a statement.

Why this question brought on a sense of shyness—or shame—wasn't clear. But it did. Heat flashed across her skin, forcing her to look away as she clenched her thighs together.

His hand slipped from her hair, cupping her cheek. "There's that beautiful blush," he said, pulling her mouth to his, pressing past her lips with his tongue, stealing her resistance in slow, sweeping licks.

When he finally released her, all she could hear was a growl. His hand returned, fisting her hair in a sharp, insistent move.

"Answer me. Use your words, sub."

Sub. The way he said it was like a summons. Demanding her obedience.

It. Was. Hot.

"Y-yes." She stuttered out her admission, the breathy word soft and weak.

As he fitted his mask back in place, she could see him so clearly now. This was Jake. She was safe. But with the single move, he became a stranger, the dangerous man in the hall. And *holy hell*, it changed everything.

"Safe word. Now," he whispered.

"Red," she choked out.

Jake's arm locked around Kathryn's waist. The move could have passed for reassuring but took on its own form of possession. She was owned whether she wore a collar or not.

Her breath hitched as his large hand made its way to palm the roundness of her butt. There, he gave her a firm squeeze, pulling her hard against him. He towered over her, every muscle of his body tensed with a predatory readiness. A hunter ready to savor his prey.

Kathryn swallowed hard.

His finger made a slow path along her inner thigh and up her skirt, tracing the sensitive line higher. Her breath quickened, keeping time with the back-and-forth motion of a touch that sizzled her skin. With each pass, Jake's finger inched closer to her core.

"You're mine, sub. Mine for the taking. Whenever and wherever I want."

Kathryn met his dark, brooding stare. By the angle of her body pressed against his, maybe her small frame was hidden from view. Maybe her heavy panting and heated moans wouldn't give her away.

Maybe . . . no one will know.

His mouth brushed hers, not possessive or rough, but a dizzying tender touch. His fingers traveled, barely skimming the sensitive underside of her ass, moving up the line between her thighs, and dipping inside her just far enough to elicit a moan.

"So fucking wet."

His finger sliced through, and she gasped. He took his time invading her body, working a second finger deep inside her. Pushing her closer and closer. Building her climax out in the open. Voices were around them. People could be heard. And if she could hear them, they could hear her.

The rustle of their steps against the pavement seem to echo across the vast lot. The people moved casually with a vague sense of purpose —leaving the building, going to their cars. Oblivious to the fact that just a few steps away, she was riding Jake's hand to the peak of pleasure.

He was claiming her. And God, she was letting him.

In that moment, Kathryn felt flushed and weak, desperately chasing an orgasm that was just out of reach. Not yet there, but quickly building. His tongue swept the line of her lips, and her gasp let him in. All the while, his fingers did their work. In and out. In. And out.

So close.

When Jake stopped, the loss was agonizing, and the loudness of her whimper was unavoidable. His mouth crashed on hers, smothering her pleading sounds.

"Don't stop," she begged. "God, please don't stop." Her body shuddered against his.

His kisses were tender as he kept her tight in his hold. "It's called a punishment for a reason, kitten."

It took a few panting breaths before Kathryn felt she could stand on her own. Watching him suck his fingers clean wasn't exactly helping, and she was seconds from finishing the job herself.

Still, his arm kept her steady against him, and his bright hazel eyes were ablaze. She hadn't come. He hadn't come. And yet, there it was. An unmistakable look. He had been dominant, stealing her will and taking control. It did something to him, and he was satisfied.

My Dom is a sadist. Him and his talented finger.

"There you two are."

Julian was heading over. Five steps away hardly gave Kathryn the precious time she needed to tug down her skirt.

"I thought you two left a while ago. Here's your phone." Julian passed it to Kathryn, then turned to Jake. "Does this mean I need to give you back your car?" He dangled the key ring from one finger, pushing out a pout as he jiggled it lightly.

Really?

Kathryn held her hand out expectantly, met by Jake's large one. He clasped her hand to his chest.

Come on . . . how far can this punishment possibly go?

"It's yours for the week. Right, Kathryn?" Jake and his smug grin were taking just a little too much satisfaction in the moment.

Seeing as I'm putty in his hands, I hardly have a choice.

"I guess so," she said with a sigh, not happy to give up the gorgeous car Jake let her drive.

"Jules, wait." Andi was making her way over from the front of the building, her strappy heels giving an already tall woman the presence of a supermodel. "Here you go. One year." She handed over a card.

He handed her one in return. "Here's my card. Ask for me. Anytime."

They exchanged a round of kisses on both cheeks before Andi departed. Jake and Kathryn said nothing but shot him expectant looks.

"Jules, is it?" Kathryn asked, crossing her arms. "True bestie or business bestie?"

She knew the drill. Only two classes of people called Julian *Jules*. Her, and an ever-growing list of business associates he wanted to connect with. Make them feel like they could offload their innermost thoughts and most of their money too. With the way the man's office had become a revolving door of Botox and filler clients, she couldn't argue with results.

"You are my only true bestie, girl. Hey, when the real Jake Russo showed up, I had to charm her somehow. I offered her all the laser hair removal her pretty body can tolerate, and maybe an injection or two. She gave me a full year's membership at Club Lazarus in exchange. What can I say? Andi's a sweetheart. A pharmacy tech by day and BDSM gatekeeper by night. That's the friend to have." Noticing Kathryn's eye roll, he added, "Don't judge. Leather and lube don't fall from trees."

Kathryn wrinkled her nose. "Andi's beautiful. She hardly needs your services."

Wounded, Julian grabbed his heart. "Kathryn Chase, if you're gonna stay my bestie, you need to get with the program. Talk like that will be the death of me. In the illustrious words of Ms. Truvy Jones, 'There is no such thing as natural beauty.'"

Leave it to Julian to quote from *Steel Magnolias*, Southern accent and all. His fascination with Dolly Parton truly knew no bounds. If Kathryn and Jake were going to get out of there before he started belting out "Here You Come Again," they'd better get a move on.

"Ready?" Kathryn asked, latching onto Jake's arm for support and trying not to squirm in place.

"Not quite. Catch you later, Julian," he said, sending him on his way. "I need to show Kathryn something out back."

"I'll bet you do," Julian said, giving Kathryn a quick peck on the cheek before quickstepping it to the car.

Glancing up at Jake, Kathryn sent up a silent prayer.

Please let it be your cock.

11
KATHRYN

The next evening, Kathryn leaned across the white linen tablecloth toward her date. "It's not that I don't appreciate it. I'm flattered. Truly, I am. But—"

Pausing, she swallowed hard as she stared at Paco. His broad shoulders filled out his expensive suit jacket to perfection, and his striking features charmed her with a look of unbridled curiosity.

It was bad enough that Jake insisted on continuing her punishment today. She'd already agreed to have dinner with Paco. A high-end place like the five-star Penrose Room hardly seemed like America's Next Top Dungeon. But it was either wear the toy Jake had insisted on, or the punishment continued for the rest of the week. And considering she had classes to teach, that would be a no-go.

Her intense reactions to the unpredictable, sporadic vibrations between her legs would be impossible to hide in front of a room of phlebotomy students. One wrong passionate cry by her while her students were practicing on each other, and harsh, inadvertent stabs were sure to follow. Drawing blood was one thing. Shanking, another.

Having dinner at this restaurant wouldn't have been Kathryn's first choice. Or her eighth. And not because she considered herself too laid-back for fine dining, but because in light of her current predicament, she knew the room would be quiet. She'd never imagined it would also be unsettlingly empty.

It was early in the evening, but not too early. The string quartet in the corner would have to play twice as loud to call themselves elevator music. And Kathryn needed a loud environment to cover her discomfort.

Clanking plates. The rumble of voices. How about a crashing glass or two?

She prayed for anything at all that would distract the ear and drown out any would-be noises. Especially the ones likely to emanate from down under. But when Paco Robles recommended a restaurant, it wasn't a good idea to put off *His Eminence*. Her only choice was to roll with the punishment and accept Paco's invitation graciously.

Buzz. Buzz. Buzz.

Kathryn couldn't enjoy the panoramic view of Colorado Springs outside the enormous picture window, though she stared at it with deep fascination.

Focus. Breathe in. Breathe out. And do not moan.

She crossed her legs tightly, wishing with all her might that the man sitting across from her didn't hear that. Abruptly, the string of tiny pulses finally stopped, just before her composure crumbled.

I can't keep this up.

"Are you all right?" Bringing his glass of chilled water to his lips, Paco sipped, studying her enough that the blush was coming whether she wanted it to or not.

"Yes. I'm fine," she said, refusing to feel guilty about that little white lie. Her heart thumped in unison with her nervous breaths. "I, uh, just remembered there's a quick text I need to send. Sorry, do you mind?"

"Not at all," Paco said, with just enough of a smile in his twinkling eyes that she suspected the worst thing possible. He knew.

Kathryn: *I'm in a meeting.*
Jake: *And?*
Kathryn: *With Paco.*

Jake: And??

Buzz.

Clenching her thighs together, she squelched whatever completely inappropriate noise was about to escape her throat, grateful that Paco was heavily engrossed in one of his favorite pastimes. The wine menu. The tall, leather-bound list spanned several pages. Enough to buy her time and quell the passing needs of what she was coming to know as Jake's sadistic Dom side.

The man was Satan. Sinful and demanding, and on the actual brink of killing her, one drawn-out orgasm at a time. Her lips pursed, tightening as she shot back another text.

Kathryn: Paco's about to lose an eye if my nipples peak any harder.
Jake: Hmm . . . several texts and no safe word. Seriously, kitten, I'm getting mixed messages.

Buzz.

She bit her tongue, preventing the tiniest yelp from growing into a full-throttle cry.

Kathryn: Yellow.

No buzz. No text. She could practically hear Jake's growl of dissatisfaction in the silence between them, but her lungs emptied with relief.

"Are you ready to order?"

The polite and courteous waiter was upbeat yet professional. He looked first at Paco before turning to Kathryn.

The last thing she needed at the moment was a spotlight. It would be a tragedy of epic proportions if another buzz zapped between her legs as the two men smiled at her. Dying of embarrassment is an actual thing.

Call it stubbornness, but she'd be damned if the word *red* was rearing its safe little head. Giving in hardly suited her deep-rooted competitive streak.

"You first," Kathryn said to Paco. Begged, really.

He closed the menu and returned it. "I'll start with the Château Lafite Rothschild."

Scanning through the selections, Kathryn caught a peek at the price. Of course, Paco immediately noticed her wide eyes, because nothing escaped the man's attention.

Would it be too much to ask that he had an off day for once? Too engrossed with his five-thousand-dollar bottle of wine to notice Kathryn was harboring a sex toy between her legs?

"Two glasses," he told the waiter, insisting with enough charm and confidence to stop any of her million objections cold.

"I've never really been into wine," she admitted shyly, not wanting to turn down Paco's generous offer, the second of the night. The first, of course, was the job offer she'd been midway through declining before the untimely interruption from her humming vagina.

At least the bullet vibrator was wedged high enough up it didn't risk sliding out. And she'd nearly lost her panty privileges today for the criminal offense of daring to almost satisfy herself in the shower. Jake had let her off easy. Ten smacks on each butt cheek. The sting of them might still be fresh, but at least her panties were intact.

"Very good," the waiter said, giving them both an attentive glance. "Did you need another moment deciding on dinner?"

Buzz.

Buzz-buzz.

"Actually," Kathryn said with a sigh, then cleared her throat. "I eat positively anything, and I trust your judgment. I really need to step *awaayyy . . .*"

Racing from the table, Kathryn took several staggering steps, lurching into the ladies' room with a loud and uncontrolled *ahhhh*. There was zero doubt that the noise she'd just released must have echoed off the marble walls of the restroom loud enough to be heard all the way out in the restaurant.

Ducking into the largest stall at the end, she slammed the door, unable to care about anything at all except the fast flutters hitting her G-spot, and Jake. With trembling fingers, she pulled her phone from her clutch.

"Call Jake."

In an even deeper timbre than his natural low tone, he answered. "Sex machine services. What's your pleasure, Ms. Chase?"

"Oh my God, Jake. Please. I can't . . . I need you . . . I have to come. I—"

The restroom door opened with an audible swoosh.

This can't be happening.

A determined set of oncoming footsteps moved slowly through the restroom. She covered her mouth, desperate to stop any chance of lust-filled noises hitting the air. She prayed the buzzing would stop, but it had a mind of its own.

Her forehead dropped against the stall's door. Biting her lip, she felt a small bit of relief from the pain, and better controlled her breathing. Her clenched legs stifled the vibrations as best they could, but at this point, her willpower was toast. Crashing waves of orgasm were upon her. Lord help whoever heard her on the other side of the stall door.

At the very edge of her orgasm, the vibration stopped. *It's like he knows.* Her disappointment emerged in an audible whimper, mourning the death of her beloved climax.

Knock-knock.

The soft, choppy knocks were just on the other side of her forehead, instantly snapping her to her senses and popping her head from the door. As if she could actually hide under the circumstances, she slid her feet softly back, taking small silent steps away from the door. *Smooth.*

Buzz.

Her body seized until she realized the latest vibration came from her phone. The one in her hand with her Master still on the line. A smile broke from her lips as she read the screen.

Jake: Open the door.

Fumbling with the damn lock that clanked through her struggle, she nearly broke it off. With a deep breath, she cracked open the door.

Faced with her Dom wearing a scandalous smile and way too many clothes for her liking, Kathryn ached for the feel of his full lips against hers, the taste of his tongue scouting every part of her mouth, and the feel of his huge cock absolutely anywhere he would put it.

"Get out here, kitten." Unconcerned that he was in the ladies' room, Jake unfastened his belt, unbuttoned his jeans, and unzipped.

"B-but—"

His brow rose as a half smile quirked his lips, skyrocketing his sexiness in seconds. "You'll do as I say or . . ."

"Or?" She hadn't moved.

"Or you'll say red."

I didn't survive three deployments to the Middle East to play it safe. And neither did Jake.

He took a strategic step back, letting her emerge from the stall and into the open. Her with her seeping wetness, and him seconds from being bare-assed and protruding. Anyone could walk in.

Why is that exciting?

Mesmerized, she watched him slide his jeans lower, catching his rock-hard cock in the palm of his hand. He stroked himself, smearing the healthy bead of pre-cum across the head. The sight of him was nearly enough to send her over the edge.

"Hike up your skirt."

She did as she was told.

"Now, turn around and pull open your blouse, but don't take it off."

With the mirror, he could see everything. Watch her from the front. See her from the back. Catch those white panties he'd insisted she wear. The plain white ones that were more sporty than dainty, and had her wondering why he'd opted for a less frilly pair.

These were a well-cut thong that flattered her figure but remained soft and comfortable. Sexy in a girl-next-door way, they paired well with her ponytail. And by the dark glare on his satisfied face, had to be completely soaked and showing every drop.

Mystery solved.

Slowly, she turned, taking her sweet time unbuttoning her blouse, because torture was a two-way street. Her hands lingered for a second across the fullness of her breasts. Her eyes locked with his in the mirror before she released the clasp, exposing her firm pink nipples.

"What if someone comes in?"

"Then we'll give them a show. Bend over," he growled.

Whatever hesitation she had was quickly snuffed out, and each time the word *red* crossed her mind, she readily flicked it away. The marble counter was icy beneath her palms, its coldness sending a shiver through her.

"Now," he said, tugging her panties down and pressing the palm of his hand across her back. "You have to relax."

She sucked in a breath and struggled, craning her neck to get another glimpse of him in the mirror.

It did little good. A second later, his reflection was out of view, hidden by her body as he sank to his knees behind her. The first lash of his hot tongue against her wetness was a tease. Several laps in, and her body rocked against him. Holding back her response was no longer an option.

Fuck it. Unless Jake suddenly decides to gag me, everyone's getting an earful.

With both his hands gripping her thighs, she tensed.

He grumbled again. "Relax."

The small vibrator was being tugged out, obviously by his teeth. And with each fraction of an inch it moved, she found herself closer to the brink.

"Oh God."

One of his strong hands pulled away just as the sleek device tugged free, making way to slide his tongue in and out, tasting her with long, intrusive licks. Her loud groan sweetened to a whimper as his tongue made its way out, and then he stood, inching into her with his dick.

"Yes," she cried out really, really loud.

Jake wasted no time. The smooth pleasure device was being worked into her other hole. Filling her. Forcing her to take him.

He was giving her everything she wanted. Making her submit.

He ran his fingers across the base of her spine, a feathery touch that made her back arch as her body shot back.

Crack. The smack on her ass was deafening and hard, ripping across her in an electric shock.

"Did I say take my cock, sub?"

Her silence earned her another slap on the ass, this one just the slightest bit harder. And louder. The pain eased to a simmer. Panting, Kathryn kept her movements controlled and still.

"No," she whispered, her chest heaving.

The low buzz lit her from the inside out with its slow, steady vibrations, setting free every inhibition and erasing every rational thought she'd ever possessed. It was ecstasy, an insatiable string of moments she prayed would never end.

"Jake, please . . ."

Another smack.

"*Please*, kitten?" he asked, as if to say *really?* Gripping each cheek harder, he squeezed them until she felt the reverberation clear from her neck to her toes. "Please what?"

It was something she hadn't asked before. She sucked in a breath, then set free the words. "Please, Master Jake."

Two slaps hit her ass cheek before his palm settled on her skin. "Please, Master Jake, what? Tell me what you want. And where you want it."

Her head was spinning, but she stayed in place. Legs spread. Breasts pressed hard to the cold marble counter. His cock teasing each building throb at her entrance. But she had to check. To know.

Kathryn craned her head ever so slightly. Her breathing stopped. The door was unlocked. *Intentionally left unlocked.*

Her voice was steady as she said it. "Fuck me." The next smack made her feel delirious. "Yes, Master Jake. Please, fuck my pussy."

"Is that what my kitten wants? Her dirty little pussy fucked? Where anyone can see?"

Her whimper had barely left her lips before he slammed the length of his dick inside, forcing the rigid thickness of himself deep in one swift move.

Her climax was instant. Her body quaked hard as she let out a deafening scream, one that must have filled the restaurant and kept on going clear to the Rockies. An ecstasy that was sure to have alerted the security staff and have her and Jake escorted from the exclusive hotel. Any second now.

Kathryn didn't care. *Couldn't* care.

It was a soft fall from paradise, toppling from a pleasurable high she'd relish for moments to come. Until being banished from the heaven of the five-star resort's ultra-posh restroom, that is.

Kathryn eyed her phone. If ever a time called for a semi-nude selfie, it was this one.

"We're not done," Jake said, not stopping. Not slowing or showing any mercy in the moment. He kept going. Thrusting. Hitting her spot over and over again.

Reaching back, she gripped the granite muscles of his thighs, digging her nails in hard as she took every last inch of him. It drove him deeper, tearing her blissfully apart.

Relentless, he slammed into her harder and faster, ramming her with angry thrusts that turned savage. Not careful or gentle, but primitive. Raw. It was her initiation. Her chance to finally meet the real Jake.

This was her Dom.

She clawed her way across his skin, letting her desperate grip carve several paths across his solid thighs, ones that were sure to leave deep, long-lasting marks. The way he needed. The way only his sub could give.

"Come again. Now!"

His guttural demand was met in an instant. He ripped another climax from her just as he took his own, collapsing his jolting body on hers. Their cries were as uninhibited as they were. The moment was everything. When Kathryn felt most alive.

"Fuck." He swept the wisps of her strawberry-blonde hair from her face to leave tender kisses on her cheek and the nape of her neck.

"I know," she said, panting.

"No," he said, chuckling as he rested his cheek against her back. "That devil pleasuring your ass. I need to shut it off." Bracing his hands against her sides, he said, "Tap my watch."

She did, clicking off the app, and the vibrations stopped. Kathryn exhaled with a satisfied sigh.

Slowly, Jake dragged himself out. With her last ounce of naughtiness, she worked her body back, capturing him in the walls of her tight pussy. After another smack on her ass, she giggled and finally unlocked her vise grip on him.

Not quite ready to move on from the small corner of luxury real estate they'd claimed as their own, she caught his reflection in the mirror. "I'm not sure I can stand."

"That's okay." Jake lifted her body and pressed it to his until she firmed up her wobbly legs. "I'll eat whatever Paco ordered for you."

"Paco!" And his ridiculously expensive bottle of wine. "I totally forgot." In a panic, Kathryn scrambled to get dressed. "Oh, I—"

"Don't worry," Jake said with reassurance.

He tugged his own clothes back in place and washed his hands. After a quick once-over in the mirror, he wrapped his arms around her, pulling her quivering body against him, and planted an unhurried kiss on her lips.

"I'll catch up with Paco while you get primped and polished, though you look absolutely perfect to me."

"I've been gone forever. He might have left."

"I doubt that. He's staying at the hotel."

"Even if he's still out there, he must have heard us, along with everyone else in this resort. Staff. Guests. Security. They're probably waiting outside, listening and enjoying the soundtrack before they cart us away."

Another warm kiss met her lips as Jake's fingers made themselves busy unbuttoning the blouse she'd managed to misalign, before rebuttoning it perfectly. "Didn't Paco tell you?"

"He couldn't tell me much of anything before my vagina started belting out opera."

"The restaurant's closed. Just for us. He knew I wanted to do something special for you, and was willing to do anything to help."

"I'm sorry, did you just say Paco splurged to have a five-star restaurant shut down to help you make me your sex slave?"

Jake's smile was absolutely diabolical. Lifting her chin with two of the naughtiest fingers in existence, he smothered her worries with a lingering kiss until her shoulders relaxed. Her own taste was still fresh on his tongue, and sucking each fluid lick through her parted lips was undoing her again.

Abruptly, he pulled away. *The tease*.

"No," Jake said with a modest grin. "Everyone already knows you're my sex slave."

That comment earned him a playful smack on the unmoving muscles carved in his chest.

With another light peck, he stepped away. "Take your time. And do what you have to do, kitten, but the bullet stays."

In my ass? Her protest was instant, but weak at best. "You can't possibly make me come at dinner."

Casually, he swung open the unlocked door. "Was that a dare?" he said as he and that cocky swagger of his strolled away.

12

JAKE

When he approached the table, Jake reached out to shake Paco's hand, but was met by a leery man with a skeptical eye.

"I can only imagine where that's been," Paco said, giving his bold red wine a wide swirl before enjoying a sip. Considering the ease of his words and the not-so-subtle smirk he wore, it was clear that Paco was enjoying this.

Jake took a seat beside him, dropping the dark linen napkin to his lap. "I'm sure your hands have done worse."

The waiter presented the wine. Jake wasn't exactly a brie and brioche sort of man, but the rules of proper table etiquette had come to him over time. High-end clients never dove into their woes without the luxuries of caviar and vintage cabernet. Finishing school was never high on his bucket list. But when his boss—a former sniper and the CEO of a multibillion-dollar conglomerate—says go do, you salute sharply with two words. *Yes, boss.*

Taking the bottle, Jake examined the label and blew out a long whistle. "You surprise me. I know you drink anything, but a fine wine guy? It doesn't seem laid-back enough for your style."

Paco took another sip of his wine, then swallowed. "I'm whatever I have to be. In a few weeks, I'll be in France. Blending into my environment is what I do best, but I need to brush up on my wines, and this one is a favorite of a client."

"Not going to class it up by swigging straight from the bottle?"

"Trust me, the night might not start with me partying my ass off like a teenager, but it always manages to end that way. You should've seen Kathryn's face when I requested a glass for her."

"I'll bet," Jake said, laughing at the thought. "Kathryn's as down-home as they get, but she'll never say no to you."

"But she did." Paco's words held the smallest hint of disappointment. He stared Jake down over the rim of his glass, narrowing his eyes. "I offered her a job."

"You're worried? Still? Scott's on the case."

Sadness washed over Paco's face. "Never send in a man to do a woman's job. The perp is good. Let's just say this case is of interest to a friend. We need to get to the bottom of this first."

The words were enough to both piss Jake off and send him into protective mode. In some ways, Paco knew Kathryn better than Jake did. Her tenacity. Her strength. Her ability to dig out the truth, no matter how many layers of subterfuge it was buried beneath.

But Kathryn Chase was also his. Jake owned her . . . mind, body, and soul. It meant more than she was his. She was his to protect.

Hands clasped, he leaned in. "Sounds like she already turned you down."

"A no now might lead to a yes. And I only had a minute with her before you took the helm." Paco lifted a brow. "Or would that be the stern?"

Not that it's his concern, but I'll be taking both before the night is over.

Jake merely shrugged. "All I know is if you're trying to woo Kathryn, fancy French wine will be about as effective as goose-liver pâté. The least you can do is offer my girl a real drink," he said with casual disregard for the high-end wine whose price tag probably ranged just below that of the man's suit.

With only a glance in his direction from Paco, the waiter eagerly hustled to his side. "Did you need something, sir?"

"Yes, Stuart," Paco said.

In his polished black vest and slacks, complete with a white button-up shirt with burgundy bow tie, all the waiter was missing was a nametag. Sure, Paco could have struck up a conversation with him—a way to kill time while Jake made himself busy thoroughly defiling his naughty little kitten. But Jake had a hunch that wasn't how Paco happened to know the guy's name.

Casually, Paco tilted his chin toward Jake, who ordered without bothering with a drink menu.

"A glass of Blanton's Gold. Neat. Two fingers."

"Nothing for Kathryn?" Paco asked, as if uncertain Jake had made the right call.

Smiling, Jake shook his head. "Like that would ever happen. I'm taking care of my girl. And I'll start with water. Should we order?"

Before Stuart could hand over a menu, Paco issued him a silent but polite dismissal. "I've got it covered." To Jake, he asked, "By the way, where is she?"

"Let me find out."

JAKE: You've got one minute before your search party arrives.
KATHRYN: I'm not sure I can face Paco.

Jake took her text in stride, pinching the bridge of his nose with an inward sigh. He handed his phone to Paco. "This from the girl who let you hook her up on a blind date in a hotel room with an unknown Dom."

Before Jake could stand, Paco's firm hand landed on his shoulder.

"I'm starving. If you go back in, who knows when you'll be out. My turn."

13

KATHRYN

The person who knocked at the ladies' room door didn't wait for Kathryn's *come in* before entering.

In anticipation of Jake, she was in the man's arms a minute too late, throwing herself right at the guy she'd been stalling to avoid.

"Well, hello again, Ms. Chase." Her purposeful wiggle to get away was no use. Rather than release her, Paco held on, squeezing her until any remaining resistance and tension evaporated. "Would it help if I said I didn't hear a thing?"

Kathryn could only smile. Pulling away, she squared up to her dear friend who had the kindest eyes and a deceptively innocent grin. "You'd do that for me?" she joked, almost ashamed for feeling uncomfortable.

"Straight-out lie to your face?" Paco gave her a reassuring kiss on her forehead. "In a New York second. But only if you get your ass out there and stop making me wait to eat. I'm withering away from hunger. And my appetite hasn't even been worked up by Master Jake."

It was her turn to play all meek and innocent. "I have no idea what you mean," Kathryn said, giggling now that she was less embarrassed, and staving off a stomach growl.

Having spent most of her nervous energy wiping down the counters and taking a snapshot or two of the large bouquet of flowers gracing the scene of the crime, she was more than ready to depart the luxurious ladies' room. Though if anyone left the hot water running a little too long, they would quickly discover a finger drawing on the mirror. One of a heart surrounding a cryptic message.

KC + JR

4

EVER

Paco didn't remove his arm from Kathryn's shoulders until he delivered her front and center to Jake, who stood ready with her chair pulled out. Scooping her into an embrace that threatened more debauchery to come, Jake pressed his lips to hers with the right amount of pressure. She couldn't hold back a small moan.

After Jake seated her, she let out a giddy squeal of glee, finding a glass of her favorite bourbon waiting front and center on her plate.

"Oh, thank God," she said, not meaning to hurt Paco's feelings. Wasting a drop of his fancy red on her admittedly unsophisticated palate seemed wrong on every level. But bourbon?

These boys better back up.

Both men laughed, and Paco held his wineglass high for a quick toast.

"Happy anniversary, you two."

His announcement sent a small surge of panic through Kathryn. She didn't recall a calendar reminder, and hadn't gotten Jake a gift. But her awkward glance at Jake was met with a cocked head and an equal amount of confusion.

Paco explained. "I believe it was four years ago to the day that a perfect angel tore a certain someone from the dark grip of death. An act that served to let him to strip and whip another day."

"Nice," Jake said before lifting his water glass, and they all brought their drinks in for a clink.

"And I'm neither perfect nor an angel," Kathryn said firmly, her insistence spurred by her latest dive into gratifying hedonism.

"You are to me."

Jake's voice carried enough of a low grumble that she shivered, barely registering his hand snagging hers or his lips pressing firmly against her knuckles. A physical response to an orgasm drought followed by the sexual equivalent of a torrential downpour.

"How about I get down to business while we eat," Paco said, "so the two of you can get down to business? Again."

Kathryn had gotten an eyeful of the steaming-hot bread, but before she could take the tiniest piece, Jake grabbed a slice and slathered it with a heaping helping of roasted garlic butter. Taunting her, he held it to her lips.

It's bread. I love bread, almost half as much as I love butter. But bread and butter? Together? The man has no shame.

Her shy hesitation was shoved aside by his playful growl, an insistent glare, and the not-so-subtle glance at his watch.

Flushed and wide-eyed, she took a healthy bite. *Not healthy like it's good for me. But healthy like if I'm going down, I'm going down satisfied.* The moan that followed, one of pure pleasure, had no chance of being held back.

"Mmm." She chewed, watching Jake take his own large bite while holding her stare.

Jeez. Is there anything this man can't seduce me with?

After teasing her with the smallest lick of his lips, he fed her another bite and set the rest of the slice onto her plate.

Definitely not.

"I enjoy a good floor show as much as the next guy," Paco said with an exaggerated eye roll, "but let's get down to the reason I really brought you here today."

Frowning, Kathryn wiped a smear of butter from the corner of her mouth. The thought of turning Paco down twisted her gut. "I'm not sure how far our talk will go."

She could feel Jake watching her, his gaze moving over her body and back up to her lips. The heat rising up her cheeks would be red-hot soon if she didn't find a distraction to cool herself down. Like work. Or pushing off Paco.

"So, this is the Troy Brooks case," she said.

"See? It's like you're already on it."

"Scott Delaney told me about it and asked me for my input. You're a long way from New York City. Why the interest?"

Paco's usual jovial smile tightened. "I can't tell you." He gave Jake a good hard stare, silently sending some message before he continued. "What's important is that we solve it first. Ahead of the police."

"Hold on. I thought I'd be working with Detective Delaney."

"And he'll think that too." Paco seemed to push past Kathryn's obvious resistance. "The stalker is good. Always a step ahead. Blending in. We need someone who blends in just as well." Setting his glass aside, he clasped his hands and leaned in. "Someone she won't see coming. An edge."

Jake held up a warning hand. "Word to the wise. Now might not be the best time trying to entice my girl with the word *edge*. And I'm a fan of Troy's too, but it's up to Kathryn. Between you and me, I'm not crazy about her going up against a psychopath. *Again*. But if she's in, it means I'm in too." His dark gaze found hers. "Not optional."

His kiss stopped her mild protest.

Paco beamed a smug smile. "Good. I get the two of you, as long as you know Kathryn gets top billing because she's the best."

"I know," Jake said, not taking his eyes off her for a moment, but acknowledging the persistent weight of Paco's stare. "Save the jedi mind tricks for Kathryn."

"I would, but she seems to be under your mind control at the moment."

To which Jake replied with nothing more than a cocked brow and a *damn straight* grin.

Turning serious again, Jake asked, "Was Troy moved again?"

Kathryn shot him a glance. *So, Jake knows about the case too.*

Paco's slight nod was pained and unsettled. "Fourth time in two days. Undercover guards at major entries. Triple-vetted all the staff. It's frustrating because we're not moving him to protect him. We're trying to catch the nut job. If we leave him in one place too long and too heavily guarded, she goes away."

"Isn't going away a good thing?" Kathryn asked.

"Not in this case. It's taken her nearly two years of building up to this level of stalking with Troy. He calls the cops, and it'll be months between contact. Which means he's on high alert, watching his back for months. This one is a little too unpredictable for my taste. But every time we move him, she resurfaces. It's more than a fleeting interest. She's in it for the long game."

"It sounds like you need a private investigator," Kathryn said after she downed a swallow of ice water. "I'm not really that type of investigator. I do insurance fraud."

"There's a difference?" Paco was casual. He pulled the bread basket closer, examining it as if the man with two-percent body fat ever indulged in a slice of bread. "If anything, you're more thorough than a garden-variety PI. With your medical background and hospital access, you can give us insights we might not readily find. Blend in better than anyone else. Using your skilled observations to sniff out the culprit without confronting them. It pays more than you make in a year, even though for you I don't think you'd consider it a job. Just a natural extension of who you are, just as much as nursing, bourbon, and bondage."

Paco's words drew a huffed chuckle from Jake.

"Plus," Paco said, "this one needs a trusted agent. And you're someone we trust."

Kathryn shrugged, schooling the smile that threatened, eyeing his pristinely tailored suit and teeing up what was sure to be an impossible challenge. "Maybe I'd do it if you actually ate a piece of bread."

"Let me get this straight," he said, cinching his lips tight. "If I eat a piece of bread, you'll take the case?"

Her eyes lit up. "Damn straight, city boy. One piece of bread and I'm all yours. And not a pansy little broken-off piece. The big, thick middle one. Right there." She pointed to the drool-worthy center slice.

Frowning, Paco peered again at the basket in question. "With butter?" he asked, not masking his disdain.

Kathryn wasn't picky. With a wide, toothy grin, she giggled. "Dealer's choice."

Removing his jacket and rolling up his sleeves, Paco seemed to be making a ceremony of eating a single sliver of bread. He buttered it lavishly. "This little morsel has to be worth my temporary ownership of one Ms. Kathryn Chase." He glanced at Jake. "No disrespect."

"None taken," Jake said, granting him permission to continue with the wave of his hand.

In one bite, Paco devoured the slice with a few moan-filled chews, then swallowed before moving on to another slice. Instead of sticking with the sourdough, this time he opted for the sweet dark rye.

"Oh my gosh." Kathryn gasped and her hand flew to her chest. "Did I convert Paco Robles to the unbridled sins of bread?"

"Hardly." He scoffed, swallowing another bite. *"Manduo, ergo curro."*

"Is that Latin for *sign me up for the bread-of-the-month club?*"

"I eat, therefore I run. Kathryn, I work out three hours a day for a reason. Pastries are my bitch. I practically devour my weight in desserts, and in many circles have the code name *Cookie Monster*. Seriously, I'm surprised you've never noticed."

"I knew that," she said. "I just thought the nickname had something to do with browser history. Tracking people on the web."

Paco popped another buttered piece in his mouth, chewing happily. "Nope." With that, he leaned back against his chair, enjoying his mouthful with an adorable smile. He took another sip of his outrageously expensive wine, lifted a brow, and waited.

Kathryn knew what he wanted. He was the same as any Dom. And if there was one thing this Dom knew how to do, it was how to get an answer to a question.

Paco needed a verbal acknowledgment. Something along the lines of *you've got it* or *I agree*. An indisputable understanding that his terms had been agreed to. In many ways, it was like the other side of Paco Robles—no different from any other transaction in corporate America.

The offer is presented, the terms are negotiated, and with his knowing presence and the unfair advantage of a dimpled chin, an acceptance secured without question.

"Fine." Kathryn blew out a breath. "Tell me where and when you want me to start, but it can't interfere with my current work with Wolfe Investigations or with my new gig at the hospital."

"Not a problem," Paco said. "I meant to ask. How's the phlebotomy class going?"

Her eyes grew wide. "You heard about that?" When she turned a questioning glance at Jake, he simply shook his head.

Paco lifted one shoulder in a shrug. "I tend to hear about everything."

I'm so dead. "I'll bet you do."

No doubt, if they kept going, Paco would start asking about everything. *How I heard about the position. How I got the job.*

Hiding facts was one thing, but outright lying about them was another. And that line was never to be crossed.

And what if Paco already knew? The man was pretty much psychic, and had his finger on the pulse of damn near everything.

Kathryn felt the unease of an uncomfortable conversation coming up. The one that steered straight toward her ex-husband. Who had insisted on dinner. It was bad enough to have Chelsea Anders in the mix. There was no way Kathryn was doubling down with an ex of her own.

That's not happening, and neither is the awkward discussion about Carter Reeves.

It was time to take the bull by the horns. Yank a hard right and steer the discussion in a completely different direction.

Kathryn's glass nearly finished, she downed the rest. Jake grabbed the waiter's attention. Politely, he gestured to Kathryn's empty glass before indicating how many. Holding up two fingers, he ordered one for himself as well.

"I'll have to do some *research.*" She drew out the word for effect, knowing it would capture Jake's attention.

It worked. There were severe penalties for topping a Dom. But desperate times called for desperate measures.

Paco took a suspicious glance around the room, looking to his left and then to his right. As if anyone could overhear them, considering the place was empty. "Don't worry. It's not the sort of research that requires you to bust into Club Lazarus under an alias."

Instinctive and outright smart, Jake glanced at Kathryn and raised his hands in mock surrender. "I didn't say a word."

With little concern, Paco explained. "I was with Jake when he got the alert on his phone."

"Of course you were." *How could I expect anything less? The man isn't just omniscient, he's fucking everywhere.* "Then maybe you know the reason my fiancé is an infamous Dom?"

Paco let out a hearty laugh, patting Jake's back as her fiancé choked on his bourbon. "Why, Master Jake. Exactly how infamous are you?" Scandal laced Paco's suggestive tone.

Prideful, Jake responded. "I'm not exactly shy, but the last thing I need is publicity, and it's not like I hired a PR firm. If Kathryn would just divulge her sources, maybe I could have some frame of reference."

"I can be a vault too," she said, shaking her head.

That and Julian would kill me. Or at the very least, he'd cut off my microdermabrasion treatments, and at this point I can't live without them. The man's touch is pure magic in the most clinical, nonsexual sense possible.

Speaking of sex . . .

"Why would you be famous as a Dom?" she asked Jake. "I'd pegged you as more of a private guy."

"First of all, *peg* has a totally different connotation in this world, and trust me, there will be no pegging. And second, there are times in a club when, well . . ." Jake took an unusually long time choosing his words. "You might want to share what you know with others. Like, a teachable moment."

Yeah, he's not getting off the hook that easily.

Hands clasped, Kathryn leaned in, prepared to learn more. "The students you have for this teachable moment. Could they be called an audience?"

"I believe the term is scening," Paco said, entirely for Kathryn's benefit.

Just the term seemed to crank the wheels in Kathryn's head. Hesitantly, she eased into her next question. "Scening. Like, a scene from a play? Performing?" Which raised yet another question. "As in . . . porn?"

When Jake's eyes met hers, she had to add, "No judgment."

It would certainly explain his moves.

"Sort of," Paco said, helpful as ever. Grinning, he took another sip of his wine.

Reluctantly, she turned her big eyes to Paco. "But all judgment aside, I'd like to think I'm up for anything, but I really don't think I could do porn."

It was Paco's turn to sputter out a laugh, and nearly snort a few hundred dollars' worth of fine wine from his nose.

Jake dove in with a few helpful clarifications. "First of all, scening is not porn."

"Are you having sex?" Kathryn asked.

"Sometimes," Jake said, tugging at his already open collar.

"Are you doing it in front of others?"

Adamant, he held up a finger. "*Not* a camera crew, if that's the question."

Paco, with an obvious wealth of expertise, inserted his own interpretation. "It's sort of an art form."

"I'm sorry, how is this artistic expression and not porn?"

When Jake and Paco exchanged uncertain glances, Kathryn picked up her phone.

"Why don't we ask Wikipedia. *Hmm* . . ." In a second, she began reading out loud. "Pornography. The portrayal of sexual subject matter for the exclusive purpose of sexual arousal. Am I warmer?"

"Fine," Jake said loudly, holding up his hands in surrender. "I'm a famous porn star."

The waiter, ready with another pour of bourbon, patted the bottle instead and set it on the table. "I'll just leave this here," he said before quickly backing away.

"If the sounds coming from the bathroom earlier are any indication, you certainly are," Paco said to Jake with a wink.

Before Kathryn could actually die of embarrassment, Jake moved her body to his lap, letting her bury her red-faced embarrassment in his shoulder.

He chuckled. "I guess that makes you a porn star too."

14

KATHRYN

"Nothing makes sense," Kathryn muttered, talking to herself. A habit she regularly indulged in, whether other people were in the room or not.

At the moment, the room she happened to be in was Jake's office. Jake, aka the cyber police, preferred any investigative work be done on his system, which required a palm print and a retinal scan. But with the types of investigations they both tended to be involved in, who could blame him?

Her fingers swiped to Scott Delaney's number on her phone. After two rings, he answered.

"Father Delaney. How may I serve?"

The man who'd recently disgraced himself by streaking past them while they were all on vacation together in Mexico, splashing them all with a cannonball, and buying a round of drinks for half the resort, was now a man of the cloth? *Fat chance.*

"Well, well, well," she said with a giggle. "There's one confessional I know to avoid."

"Nonsense, my child. I've heard it all."

"That's what scares me. I'm, um, not on speakerphone, am I?"

Scott's tone turned serious. "No."

"Good. I need the police report from the night Troy was shot. I got his medical records from admissions."

"Do I want to know how you got them?"

"Toss an investigative nurse in the middle of a hospital, and the answer is no. You don't want to know."

"Glad I didn't ask. I'll have someone send you the report. What email?"

"K at Russo Investigations dot com."

"Something wrong?" he asked.

Kathryn heard the strain in Scott's voice. It was always stressful when a lead detective caught on to the poorly hidden fact that you weren't ready to share a hunch.

Instead of misleading him with something lame like *just checking something out*, or a flat-out lie, Kathryn answered honestly. "I don't know."

"Understood." Disappointment colored his response.

"Scott," she said earnestly, "I don't know now. But I'll tell you the moment I do."

"Hey." His tone lightened. "I know you will. Do what you do best."

Kathryn saw the email notification. "It's here."

"I'll let you go." Scott cleared his throat. "Yes, go. Go with God, my child."

~

"According to this," Kathryn mumbled to herself as she pored over the police report, "the assault happened outside a club."

A night club, she assumed.

"By the descriptions, it could almost be Club Lazarus. But with a blood-alcohol level that high . . . he arrived at the club only an hour before the attack. How could he have a blood-alcohol level that borders on *gag on your own vomit* sort of drunk that fast?"

"Planning a wild night?" Jake asked, popping his head in.

Embarrassed, Kathryn felt her cheeks warm. "Just researching the case with Troy."

Jake interrupted her for a kiss. If his mouth nibbling hers didn't kick her pulse into high gear, the tight jeans and leather jacket he was wearing were sure doing the trick. The bright Colorado sun in the rich blue sky meant Jake and the other woman in his life were going for a ride.

"Enjoy Cecilia," she said, referring to his Harley. "Hey. Is it true there's no alcohol served at any clubs? Like Club Lazarus."

Jake nodded. "It slows a person's responses. Makes them more tolerant to pain, and less likely to use their safe word if and when they need to."

"What if someone brought in their own?"

Jake stroked the scruff of his chin. "Too risky. If the person is caught, it's one of the quickest ways to get tossed out. Their membership would be revoked right away, and they'd be blackballed."

Kathryn poked around in the pencil cup on the desk, bypassing six other pens before finding a bright purple one to take notes. *It couldn't have been Club Lazarus.*

"I have purple pens?" Jake asked, amused.

"Pink ones too."

"You, uh, sure you don't want your own office?" He chuckled, picking up a pen with a sparkly unicorn on top.

Kathryn gave him a resigned shrug. She'd take one if she had to. But with Jake gone so often, it was the one place that screamed Jake everywhere she looked. And the smell of his leather executive chair . . . one whiff, and it was like he was there. It had crossed her mind more than once to have her way with that leather.

His lips tickled her smile. "My office is your office. But would it kill you to leave your panties around?" The man in the dangerous jeans cupped her cheeks and left her one lasting kiss. "See you in a few. Call if you need me."

Once he left and the temperature of the room lowered to a reasonable level, Kathryn got back to work, comparing reports from the police and the hospital.

Breathalyzer . . . clean?

Scrolling through years of police reports on Troy, Kathryn stopped. Breathalyzer installed in his car . . . clean. A dozen instances of being pulled over by the police for suspected DUI, and every time clean. But on two occasions requiring hospitalization, including this one, a blood draw revealed blackout-drunk levels of alcohol.

Her vision blurred. After rubbing her eyes, she was ready for a break. A minute or two researching the BDSM world—definitely *not* looking at porn—might perk her up. Within a few sites, research was about to take on a whole new meaning.

Seriously, some of this shit should have an ARE YOU REALLY SURE? disclaimer on it. When a website asks if you're eighteen—as required by every single splash page before she could proceed—it should mean you're ready to see what's on said screen. Maybe they could give you a visual warning with a nude image or two. A provocative pose. The scandal of a reverse harem.

As with all her research, Kathryn was sure she'd seen it all. From a medical perspective. And this, she convinced herself, was medical research.

After all, I'm a nurse. A damn good one. How kinky can it be?

From Jake's private compound high on a Colorado mountain, the good thing was that no research was off-limits. Which also happened to be the bad thing. There are rabbit holes, and there are rabbit holes. And these were definitely not her mama's rabbit holes.

One woman was decked out in clamps like a Christmas tree, with every erogenous zone of her body pinched. Earlobes. Nipples. The three at her hoo-hah made Kathryn shut her eyes tight, recapture her bravery, and look again in jaw-dropping disbelief. Staring, she couldn't get over the woman's smile. She looked satisfied. Content. Maybe even refreshed.

Polite pass. I think.

She wondered what a real threshold would be for her. *At what point will I have to use my safe word?*

Kathryn's attention turned to a YouTube link. The word *fire* got her attention, and paired with *B-D-S-M* sounded intriguing. *Click.*

A woman with bright red lips was bound to a bench, not the exact type Kathryn had sat on in Club Lazarus, but similar. A series of flaming wands tapped along the bare skin of her back, touching her for moments at a time. All the while, she lay there, moaning.

Kathryn searched around Jake's desk. Her preference sheet had to be here somewhere. It didn't take much shuffling, and Jake would definitely know she'd moved his cheese, but she found it.

Could she imagine herself in the woman's place, with a blazing wand lightly pounding along her back? It wasn't exactly turning her on, but being touched by fire intrigued her.

I'm not a pyromaniac, I'm just interested.

She ignored the cautious little voice in her head and scanned the form.

Hmmm. That sort of kink seemed to be missing. Moving lower, she checked the little box next to OTHER and wrote on the line FIRE PLAY.

At the bottom of the screen, a few images caught her eye. They were the sort of easy-click, instant-buy products that others with a fire fetish seemed to have purchased. She didn't have much interest in the outfits, toys, or assortment of piercings, but a few pieces caught her eye. Things like horse-riding gear, leashes, restraints of an imaginative range, and collars.

Why hasn't Jake given me one? Maybe it's only for a club? Or a scene?

Jake Russo owned every part of her and had topped it off with an engagement ring. Was a collar really that important? Fighting the impulse to buy one for herself—which sort of defeated the purpose—Kathryn didn't care what links she clicked next, but she had to move on.

Click.

It took her a second of staring at the screen to realize she hadn't accidentally happened upon a crafting site. Instead, she'd entered the world of bondage.

Shibari. Kinbaku. Silk. Jute. Cotton. A rainbow of colors that made her insides dance with delight. Fire play might have been intriguing, but it was these two little words that ignited an inferno between her legs and in her soul.

Rope play.

If love at first sight existed beyond Jake, it was this. Beautiful, ornate, elegant knots that bound a sub, keeping her, or him, in their place.

There were dizzying variations on the subject. Sometimes bent over, the submissive would be secured with her arms behind her back. Sometimes spread-eagle, with the arms winged against the bent legs, and tied together to be taken. Or tamed. Bound in a hog-tie was a common image, where every so often the sub was gagged.

There was a small population of criminal activity that might enjoy Kathryn's inability to speak, since her testimony often resulted in their new life behind bars.

I've been gag-ordered, but never actually gagged. Would I like it? Would Jake?

And then there were the suspensions. Amazing Cirque du Soleil-like feats where the sub was tied and hanging in beautiful poses that should probably be reserved for gymnasts and stunt doubles.

The more Kathryn looked, the harder it was to look away. The elegant knots spoke to her in ways nothing else did. Being bound. Forced to submit. Taking everything she was given. Her pleasure or punishment at the sole discretion of her Dom. Why was that unbelievably hot?

But it was also the ropes themselves that were alluring. The deep reds, royal blues, and wine shades of purple made the bindings their own intricate works of art. They were beautiful. Richly colorful. And . . . familiar.

Where have I seen those before?

Kathryn clicked back to the police report. This time, she double-clicked on the attachments, focusing on the photographs.

Studying the images closer, she struggled. This was a damn good lead.

She blew out a frustrated breath, flipping between photos of the shibari knots and Troy's last attack. In those images, there were unusual imprints on his skin, similar like those left by shibari knots. But no ropes. It was like wishing for a downpour from a raindrop or two. Maybe this wasn't about Troy.

I've seen these ropes before.

Frustrated, she shot up and paced.

But where? A website? Netflix?

She fidgeted with some stray strands of her hair, flicking them between her fingers before tucking them behind her ear.

A grocery store? Or a gas station? Maybe a home improvement store?

She and Jake had started building a raised vegetable garden in the back. And every home improvement store was fully stocked with all sorts of rope. But only in neutral colors, most being rough-textured and industrial-strength.

No. That's not it.

Exasperated, she huffed, stopped in place, and shut her eyes.

Red. The ropes I've seen are rich shades of cherry red.

She couldn't lay her finger on why this was important, but it was. It took Kathryn several more laps across the length of the office to dislodge the memory, but it worked. She let out a small gasp.

Here. I've seen them right here.

Kathryn rushed through bookmarking the pages and saving them to her favorites on the browser before making her way down the long flight of stairs and to the expansive bay of the garage.

With Cecilia gone, left behind in the oversize ten-car garage were three other equally impressive motorcycles, two sports cars, and an assortment of rugged trucks and SUVs, an extension of Jake's masculine presence in every leather seat and chrome accent.

A small smile emerged. The man was everywhere.

She stood, staring at the closed cabinet, remembering the last time she'd stood there.

The memory was sharp and vivid, and ripped open the wound of seeing yet another side of Jake. The cold, dark tower of a man whose tormented hazel eyes barely recognized who she was. It was then that Kathryn understood Jake could be dark. Even dangerous, according to him.

I nearly lost him that night. Again.

But it was within these cabinet doors that she'd happened upon the ropes. Even without looking inside, she could envision them, tied in neat bundles, hung on a tidy row of hooks.

Her fingers paused in brief hesitation before she pulled open the cabinet door.

There they were, exactly as they were left the last time she saw them —an assortment of alluring cherry-red ropes she'd mistaken for mountain-climbing equipment. Which made perfect sense. After all, they were in Colorado. And lived high on a mountain.

Leaning closer, she inspected the ropes again, this time looking with more than her eyes. With two fingers, she traced the fine, smooth fibers, following the lines to a single knot holding the bundle in place. She could feel something tightening around her heart.

Have others been in these ropes? How many subs has he had? Has he tied all of them up? All of them except me?

The tempting bundles dangled from various hooks, but it was the knot that caught her eye. She pulled one down, cocking her head as she lightly traced the knot, memorizing its structure as she untied it. She wanted to know him. This part of Jake. To understand him better.

Kathryn wasted no time unraveling the bundle before winding a length of it around her wrist. Then she held out a longer length like a jump rope and flipped it over her head, letting it fall to her butt. With the rope low around her ass, she pulled, satisfied that a rope this size could hold her up.

Cirque du Soleil, here I come.

15

KATHRYN

"So, how's the case going?" Paco asked, his voice on speaker, but Kathryn searched for the right words to answer.

Busying herself with the deep-red length of rope, she completed several successive knots, the result looking almost as if a flower had bloomed from her hands.

Beautiful.

Pleased, she tightened it a little around her thigh, and the deep cherry color of the rope became the perfect garter. The color was a beautiful contrast to her fair skin, and she hoped Jake would like the look of it against her light freckles.

"Like I'm a hamster on a wheel, and no matter how fast I move or how determined I am, I end up at the same place," Kathryn said, a little annoyed as she worked another part of the rope, twisting it, but not quite mastering the look she'd seen on the YouTube video she was watching.

Muting the video on her iPad, she gave Paco her full attention, fiddling with the length of rope to keep her hands busy.

"Did Troy Brooks drink? Like, heavily?"

"He claims he doesn't. It was one of the conditions of his contract because he's a recovering alcoholic. No team would touch him without that clause. But you're hitting on a speedbump in the case. His car won't start unless he uses a Breathalyzer. It's always clear when he drives to his locations, but his blood alcohol is through the roof an hour later, when he's found. Seems physically impossible."

"If he wanted to get drunk fast, there are ways," she said. "None that are pleasant. In fact, most are life threatening. Can't we just ask him?"

"Under the advice of his attorney, he's clamming up."

Surprised, Kathryn paused. "Even with you?"

"Don't mistake my interest in this case for a friendship with Troy. I'm protecting the interests of another party. A community, you could say. Anyway, Scott said you requested pics. He's only allowed to distribute certain ones, even to you. I can get you any others you might need."

"The ropes. If you have more images of the ropes and knots from his first kidnapping attempt, it would help," Kathryn said, now unknotting what she'd done so she could start again. Backing up the footage on her iPad, she picked up at the critical knot-tying point of the YouTube video.

"Let me dig through the stockpile and send you everything I have. Is there anything else you need?" Paco's all-knowing smile had a way of beaming through the speaker on her phone.

I could use any blueprints you have to figure out this frigging knot.

Kathryn huffed in despair. "Okay, Fort Knox, how about you give it to me straight. We've known each other a long time. The cops have always brought me all the way in on a case, and now I'm having to go through you because you have photos that they don't. A pro basketball player is mildly drugged, and somehow a woman who he claims he doesn't know was able to subdue him. A drug that apparently spikes his blood-alcohol reading? Feel free to let me in on what's really going on."

Paco pulled in a breath before answering. "I'm protective about this community." The seriousness of his tone caused Kathryn to stop fiddling with the ropes and listen. "People who play in this world—our world—are vulnerable. Exposing themselves more completely then they ever otherwise would. I might have taken extra precautions where I don't need to."

"I understand." And in the same way that she had been privileged with the confidence and privacy needs of the patients she'd served, she did. "It's okay. You don't have to tell me everything."

"But I do. Because if I don't, you could miss something. Something that might be important. Something that everyone else has probably already missed."

Silently, Kathryn agreed. "Is this one of those situations where if you tell me, you have to kill me?"

"If that were the case, what method would you prefer for your demise?"

Without batting an eye, the answer was automatic. "Death by chocolate."

"That was fast."

"I've thought this through. A sugar coma of delectable dark chocolate seems to be the way to go. Seriously, you can tell me anything, Mr. Robles. Nuclear codes. What's really going on in Area 51. Who D. B. Cooper really is. I'll keep it all locked up tight."

Paco explained a little more about Troy's background, giving Kathryn the excuse to resume her fascination with knots. "Troy made one of those rookie mistakes that I was worried about you making. He put an ad on Craigslist."

"For what?"

"For a sub."

Her fingers stopped abruptly as she tried to process this.

Troy was an epic celebrity. A professional basketball player. She understood the stigma that would go along with this information getting out.

Hell, Kathryn had been worried about bumping into Andi at the club. What she must have thought. What it meant as part of the dynamic of their teacher-student relationship. And that was just one person. It wasn't as if the whole world was watching, like it would be with Troy.

It pissed Kathryn off and made her wish she could grab a newspaper and take out a full-page ad that had only two words on it. *No. Judgment.*

Paco told her more, sharing details about Troy's attack. Her hunch was right. It was outside a club. Kathryn only gave half her attention to her next knot.

Her head shook slowly with realization as she tackled a particularly difficult knot to blow off a fraction of her steam. "That's why he's in the ropes. It wasn't a kidnapping attempt. He was a willing participant . . . maybe a switch? Or at least at some point he was. So, he knows who it is."

"Partially true. It was consensual to a point, until she attempted to drug and kidnap him. And he has no idea who she is. A petite woman with no distinguishing marks, average weight, average height. A wig and colored contacts that changed each time they met, completely transforming her look. Hell, for all he knew, they were completely different women. He was naive enough to think that his brute strength would protect him from a total stranger."

"He should know men can be outsmarted or overpowered by a woman. The show *Snapped* should be mandatory viewing. Does his girlfriend know?"

"She does now. Making the breakup partially true too. She needs time to process it."

"Process it? Or kick his ass for not telling her the truth."

"A little of both. She still loves him. Even accepts him. Just taking a good long look at what this means and what she's really in for."

Kathryn studied the knots covering several areas along her legs. "Join the club."

With the ropes binding her like a dark cherry web, Kathryn bent forward, securing one of the last knots with her teeth, tightening the hold as best she could. Which was pretty good as far as she could tell.

Both of her upper arms were tethered to her sides, with her wrists and hands mostly free. She'd also managed to anchor her forearms to her thighs, under-weaving the rope in roughly the same spots the video had pointed out.

Her iPad had gone black, and it was just out of reach. As was her phone.

Shit. How do I get out of this?

"Um, Paco, can I call you back?"

"Everything all right?" he asked, because he was freaking clairvoyant.

Should I ask for help?

"Everything's fine." Straining her arms upward, she meant the forceful move to give her arms just enough room to pull free. But when the motion had the opposite effect, tightening the rope around her, she decided to bury her shame and ask Paco for advice. "Uh—"

"Okay, I'll call you tomorrow." The line disconnected.

Dammit.

Kathryn gave a mournful look at the clock and icons staring back up at her from the home screen of her phone.

The ropes were definitely tightening with each pull, so she stopped. If she wasn't careful, parts of her hands, wrists, arms, or legs risked falling asleep. But the thing that always stayed awake was her nervous bladder. Unless she was prepared to wet herself all over Jake's office chair, she had about two hours max to figure something out.

Call Jake?

It was always an option, but these were his ropes. They were private, apparently. She and Jake had lived together for months. If he'd wanted to share them with her, he would have, but he didn't.

Maybe that said something about their relationship as a whole, or his trust in her.

And as she'd rifled through his cabinets, mucked around with his ropes, and might have actually considered cutting them with the scissors that remained thankfully out of reach, who could blame him? Kathryn hadn't exactly earned her pass on the two-way street called Trust.

When her phone screen went black, panic set in. She'd wasted five whole minutes thinking through this, which meant five minutes less time to keep Jake's chair pee-free.

"Alexa? Call Spouse."

"*Okay.*"

16

KATHRYN

*O*nly through the ninety percent willpower and ten percent not wanting to get caught in this embarrassing situation had Kathryn managed to figure a way out of her current predicament. Without calling Jake. Strumming her fingers along her legs—the ones she was knotted to—she passed the eternity of time until her rescuer arrived mentally rummaging through the pages on his desk.

There was a corner of a receipt that she'd ignored the first few passes, but now zeroed in on, making out a single word at the top. *Jewelers.*

A jewelry store? With her lips and nose, she managed to slide several pages covering the small receipt to the side. The sum total at the bottom of the receipt had to rival that of a car. Or her engagement ring.

A reminder popped up from Jake's system. The word KITTEN was too alluring to pass up.

Punishment be damned. I'm going in.

Shamelessly, Kathryn bowed to press her nose to double-click the mouse, first opening the invitation, and then the attachment. The architectural drawing that opened up wasn't what she expected. It was, for the most part, a big black box with sleek lines. Five stories tall with dark glass surrounding the three highest floors.

A dark, haunting building, it looked like it could have been designed by Peter Zumthor. Beautiful and elegant, it reminded her of Kunsthaus Bregenz, a building that she'd obsessed over for years that was home to a museum in Austria. It ranked at the top of her bucket list, next to Zambia and Fiji. If the drawings were for a secure facility, it was one hell of a posh one.

"Yoo-hoo!" came a booming voice.

Startled, Kathryn hurriedly reshuffled the pages on the desk with a few hearty blows, and smashed her nose into the mouse to clear the screen. *Traces of snooping—gone*.

Her partner in crime had unfettered access to the place, to come and go as he pleased. Which happened to be the same person who would both have her back, and under the right circumstances, disavow any knowledge of her. But he didn't need to see this. And if any part of that receipt was showing, he'd notice.

"Up here," she shouted.

The loudness of several heavy steps closed in on her just in time. Kathryn wiggled her fingers, staving off the climbing pins and needles. Her arm was falling asleep, and her bladder was giving her warning signals.

"Where?" he called out, sounding farther down the hall.

"Over here," she called out, her tone ringing of guilt. "In Jake's office."

Though Julian walked to the door, he made barely a step inside before halting to a dead stop. Her threatening squint, along with the loud long huffs shooting from her nostrils, should have been enough of a warning for him to tread lightly. They weren't.

Rather than rush to her rescue, her best friend held up his phone.

She heard several clicks, and then the silence of what had to be video mode. Julian prowled around her with slow, calculated strides. Paparazzi filmmaking at its finest. Even from behind, she could hear the snickers—the *oohs* and *oh yeahs*—as he captured every square inch of the bind she was in, wrapped and knotted like a shibari birthday gift.

"Julian," she said with equal parts fury and bashful pleading. "You know I'm going to kick your ass as soon as I'm free."

"Ha," he said. "Big talk from a woman decked out in macramé. It's like knitting gone wrong. But at least you're dressed."

"Dressed? What does that have to do with anything? We're both nurses. You might not be straight, and I know boobs are a gay man's kryptonite, but you can't tell me a little nudity would keep you from helping me."

Julian pondered her words as he continued filming. "Help you, yes. But I wouldn't have been able to get all this amazing blackmail material if you were nude. It's fucking fabulous." He zoomed in on her face. "True confession—exactly how bad were you, you dirty little girl, to get punished like this? And how long has Jake left you here?"

Regret filling every inch of her body, Kathryn let her head fall forward with a sigh, building up the strength for the moment of truth. "Jake didn't do this."

Clasping the phone to his chest, Julian glared at her as his voice shot up an ear-piercing two octaves. "You'd better not be cheating on my man, Jake!"

Kathryn gave her best friend of a decade a deadpan look. "Look, Sherlock, let's get a few things straight. First of all, Jake is *my* man, so keep your mitts to yourself and your fantasies locked away."

Waggling his brows, Julian huffed out, "Fine. I won't tell you about any of my smoking-hot firefighter dreams."

"Got my own, thanks. And second, I would never, ever, not in a million years, cheat on Jake. Not only am I not a cheater, but he has more stamina than an entire stable of thoroughbred stallions, causing me to tap out on more than one occasion. And third, *if* I were the cheating type, I'd sure as hell be smart enough, and respectful enough, not to do it in the man's own damn home."

After two seconds of a stare-down, Julian leaned in, hushing his tone. "Are you saying you're in a thruple? No judgment." His eyes widened as he anticipated her response.

Exhausted and still unable to wriggle her way free, no matter how much she tried, Kathryn blurted, "For the love of God, Julian, I did this to myself."

He lifted a brow as he eyed the ropes. Remorseful, he shook his head with a pathetic *you poor dear* look of pity. "Worst cry for help ever."

"So much for no judgment," she said, scoffing while barely holding back a laugh. "I was trying something I saw on YouTube and got stuck. Just help me get out of these."

Julian pocketed his phone and reached out to help. Tugging at an extra-tight knot, he asked, "Why didn't you call Jake?"

She cringed. "Because I didn't want him to know I've been messing with his stuff."

Julian's busy fingers stopped at those words, and he took two large steps back. "We have now come to the point in the conversation where we discuss payment."

Helpless, Kathryn asked, "What do you want?"

"Dinner."

Easy enough. "Done."

"In Vail."

There was always a catch.

Of course. The high-end ski resort. The one he always wants me to go to, but the reality of me and my clumsy ass on skis forces my repeated decline.

"Fine," she said with a huge sigh. "You've got me over a barrel. Just hurry up before Jake gets home."

"Too late," said the low, disapproving voice at the door.

Looking up, Kathryn shrank a little inside her own skin. The thundering of her heart left her breathless, frozen in place. Her voice caught in her throat, weak as she stumbled over half-formed words and met his hard stare. The storm of Jake's dark hazel eyes.

With his arms crossed, every tight muscle was strained as he looked down, working his way across her body. It wasn't the ropes that made her feel trapped and caught. Heat rose in her cheeks, along with the plea of forgiveness in a bashful smile.

"Julian," Jake said, never moving his hungry gaze from hers. Without looking down, he fished out his wallet and held up his black card. "Dinner's on me if you're out of my house in under one minute."

Snatching the card and hurrying out, Julian asked over his shoulder, "What's my budget?"

"Paris. Now get the fuck out of here."

How Kathryn heard the pounding of Julian's fast-paced steps over her own heartbeat was a mystery. But she heard them echoing down the stairs, through the house, and straight out the front door. For all she knew, Julian would be in France in time for dinner.

Abandoned, she was left with nothing but her runaway pulse, her panting breath, and Jake's smoldering gaze as he scanned every square inch of her. For as well as she knew this man and those eyes, the intensity of this stare was different.

Raw. Penetrating. Dark.

The feel of her own clothes burned beneath his stare. She needed them off. *Now.* If only she could talk. Her weak attempts started as whimpers, which erupted in a moan as she struggled ineffectively against the ropes.

In two long strides, Jake towered over her as he looked down with menacing desire and enough of a devilish half smile, her whole body shivered under his penetrating gaze. He leaned in, locking his hands on the arms of the chair as he reclined it. From some deep spot in his chest, he grumbled low with a sound of pure approval.

"Playing with string, kitten?"

Her indecisive words stopped short as he retrieved a knife from his desk's bottom drawer. A six-inch blade.

"Don't know?" he asked when she couldn't come up with an answer. Two fingers slipped between different areas of rope and skin. "Don't move."

As if that is even possible.

In a sharp burst, he sliced the rope, freeing a small part of her wrist. "Too tight," he muttered as he set the blade back on his desk.

If Kathryn could make a noise, she'd be stammering. But despite her mouth opening and closing several times in a row, no words came out.

Nothing but a few desperate huffs, followed by a lick, a bite of her lower lip, and pure anticipation of his lips landing on hers any second now.

Instead, Jake's cruel mouth moved past her ready one, a breath away from her ear. Low and growling, he asked, "Is this what you need?"

Slamming her eyes shut, she realized she didn't know. Wasn't sure. *Yes? Maybe?*

"You're not answering," he murmured against her neck.

"I . . ." She paused as the heat of his mouth moved across her breast, penetrating her thin bra like a hot knife through butter. There was no way to get free. Nothing she could do. She was trapped. His captive. Forced to submit. "I don't know," she lied. His mouth moved across her body, and she soaked in every heated breath.

His fingers slid between her legs, beneath her soaked panties, and sliced a straight line up across her folds. Waiting for them to make their way inside her was no use. He pulled them away.

"*Ahh*," she cried. Her nipples tightened. Her entire body clenched, aching and desperate for relief. She needed him. Needed more . . . more . . . more.

Jake painted her own wetness across her lower lip, then licked it off before letting her suck away what little remained on his tongue. "Your ready little pussy says otherwise. Yes or no, kitten? Or do I have to paddle it out of you?"

"Paddle?" Her voice cracked as her wide eyes met his devilish ones.

He arched a brow. "So, you like that idea too?"

Kathryn pushed past her panting enough to give several vigorous nods, but Jake shook his head.

"Not good enough."

He took a step back, saying the words with almost callous disregard for the flurry of heat building within her. The weeping between her thighs. The raw need to have him. *Now.*

"Please," she begged.

"Please?" He let the word fall flat between them. "Please won't cut it this time."

Ripping his shirt over his head and removing his pants, he revealed every line and curve of his cut abs and carved thighs, freeing his hard, jutting cock. The naked man before her again dimmed his gaze, hardening it in a way that struck her core like flint against steel.

"For the next hour, only three things can move past your lips," he said gruffly as he moved in. "Yes, sir. Your safe word. And my cock. Do you understand?"

She barely managed to answer with a staggered breath. "Yes, sir."

His hard gaze fell on her, its intensity filling her core with heat. When he tightened his grip on her hair, her mouth opened in response, and he pushed his hips forward until his dick touched her lips. Her tongue tasted the savory wetness of his strained tip, giving it several long licks.

"Take more," he said, driving her mouth to swallow his staff, but not all the way. With one hand guiding her head, he gave her just enough that she ached for him in the back of her throat.

Sucking hard, she craved him. More of him. *All* of him.

Her body rocked, taking in every thrust and movement of his thighs and hips, restricted only by the tethers of the ropes. This was a dominance. A freefall into submission where her surrender was unconditional, leaving behind nothing but whimpers and hums against his cock.

Her nails dug into the arms of the chair. She gripped and fought for his release more than her own. The deeper she sucked him in, the more he let go. She drove the pace and depth. Kathryn controlled the rhythm. But Jake controlled her.

"That's it, kitten. Make me come."

Another few thrusts, and his groans became long and strained, cutting through the air as the heat of his climax emptied into her throat.

His release was bittersweet against a storm of desire that tightened her nipples and ached in her core. She wanted her clothes off and the ropes gone, but she'd settle for satisfaction. And she didn't care how she got it. If it meant dry-humping the full-grain leather on his high-back chair, she was getting it, and she was getting it soon.

Kathryn twisted her arms, desperate to be free.

"Did I say you could move?"

She froze.

"Spread your legs."

She inched them open, and Jake's lips curled, but not into a smile. His expression was far too sinister for that. He leaned over, speaking to the skin of her neck as she felt him unbutton her shirt.

"Wider," he said, nipping her neck. "And what do you say?"

At his words, she forced her thighs apart, stretching her denim shorts in a vain attempt to expose herself. "Yes, sir."

Jake reset several knots, undoing and refastening them. Creating works of art as he secured her legs to the arms of the chair. He was hard again. And he continued taking his sweet damn time.

Torturing me.

"Don't. Move." In an instant, Jake painted on a remarkably evil grin and left the room.

Actually left. The. Room.

What in the actual fuck? An uncontrolled, blood-curdling scream flew from her lips. "Reddddd!"

Nothing but Jake's hand appeared in the door with a blindfold dangling from it. "You sure about that?" Not waiting for a response, he swaggered back in. "I didn't think so."

With a single swift move, he reclined the chair before covering her eyes. The cool satin cloaked her in darkness, amplifying each sensation as much as the dominant rumble of his voice. His words were hot against the insides of her legs. "Have you had enough?"

"Yes," she said with a sigh.

"*Hmm?*"

"Yes, sir," she said, tensing so she didn't squirm.

A coldness touched her thigh, just below the leg of her shorts, and she heard the rip of the cloth as it was cut from her body. With two more swift slices of the blade, her panties were gone.

Kathryn shivered, thrilled at the knife play. *Should I add that to my preference sheet?*

All rational thought was swept away as two fingers teased her entrance, then pressed in and out as his tongue swiped her clit. And then it was gone, replaced by the full thrust of his hard cock, pounding hard as his grip tore into her thighs.

If he's not careful, he'll break the chair. Me and the chair. But I don't want careful. I want more. And that's saying a lot considering the man is balls deep, and I can feel the full thickness of him from my spread-eagle thighs to the back of my throat.

"Is my kitten ready to come?"

No. Ready was an hour ago. Kitten is about to explode.

But all she could utter, breathy and pleading, were the words, "Yes, sir."

"Not until I say," he said firmly, thrusting hard enough to light every cell in her body on fire.

Even behind the blindfold, her eyes slammed shut. Kathryn tensed, trying anything to avoid falling over. Biting her lip. Holding her breath. Her body was on the brink of shattering into a hundred million pieces.

Jake slammed into her, over and over, until nothing else mattered—nothing existed but her racing heart and the wild sensations coursing through every part of her body at once. And him.

"Now!" he cried out as their orgasms collided, tearing her so completely apart in the strongest climax of her life.

17

KATHRYN

*R*esearch.

Kathryn repeated the mantra over and over again in her mind as she and Julian strolled through the jewelry shop's door, mentally reinforcing the little white lie as she muttered, "All I'm doing is research."

"If this is the kind of research you usually do, sign me up. All I can say is Daddy likes."

Julian was more than a little excited to be there. With his wide eyes scanning each and every brightly lit case, Kathryn could only pray he'd be able to keep his raging hard-on in check.

"Down, boy."

"Welcome to Hayes Fine Jewelers," the well-dressed clerk said. His scrutinizing gaze pinged between the two, quickly surmising who was the decision-maker as he turned toward Kathryn. "My name is Anthony. I'm here to help you find the next love of your life."

"Actually, Anthony," Kathryn said, sliding a tight arm through Julian's and leaning into him. "My husband here wanted to buy me an exquisite piece of jewelry—"

Eager to play along, Julian said, "It's our anniversary! Ten years, and we haven't killed each other yet." He drove home the idea that they were married by swatting his little lady firmly on her ass.

The only reason he still had that hand was because that was his right hand, and by extension his livelihood. If she took Julian from his duties as head nurse at a premier plastic surgery institute, it would mean an eternal damnation of never hearing the end of it and forever buying his drinks.

Back to the task at hand.

"But I had something in mind," Kathryn said. "Something special. Similar to a piece you sold a friend of mine just the other day." Her voice lifted, and she batted her eyelashes.

"We pride ourselves on the confidentiality of our clients," the salesclerk said low.

"Money's no object," Julian said proudly.

Anthony's reserved smile widened to a toothy grin. "Many of our pieces are custom and one of a kind, but I'll see what I can do. Who is your friend?"

Nervous, Kathryn lowered her voice. It cracked a little as she said, "Jake Russo."

Anthony's face lit up. "Of course! Any friend of Mr. Russo's is a friend of mine."

"Show us what he bought," Julian said a little too eagerly. When Kathryn elbowed him gently in the ribs, he hushed a yelp under his breath and cleared his throat. "If you would, my good man," he said, correcting himself in an atrocious British accent.

Anthony began leading them through the store. "Unfortunately, that was a custom piece. An unrivalled one-of-a-kind. I'm afraid I don't have anything remotely like it at the moment, but we could always custom make something similar, but uniquely to your liking."

Abandoning his faux British accent for a decidedly Australian one, Julian requested a look-see at something else. "What's the closest thing you have to what Mr. Russo purchased, mate?"

"One moment." Anthony moved through the store, a sense of purpose to his steps.

Kathryn gave Julian a semi-stern talking-to, smirking as she narrowed her eyes. "Best friend status, A plus. Community theater, D minus. The only way your acting could get any worse is if we added a top hat and a monocle."

Julian busted out a cockney accent this go-round. "That's right harsh, Guv'ner. Bustin' on me accent and trying to dress me like Mr. Peanut."

Kathryn couldn't help letting out a loud laugh that echoed across the store. She quickly covered her mouth, meekly apologizing to a few snooty and disapproving patrons, as well as the sales staff who didn't mind at all, based on their pasted-on smiles.

"Here we are."

Anthony and a sales associate presented them with a blinding array of diamonds on a black velvet pillow, along with a silver tray holding three flutes of champagne.

"Happy anniversary, Mr. and Mrs. . . ." Anthony's question lingered in the air as he handed the flutes around.

Uh-oh. They hadn't exactly run through their back story, or even their fake names.

"Bond," Julian blurted. "James Bond. But my friends call me Jimmy. And my wife—"

Kathryn shot him a hateful glance, her expression clearly conveying *Mention a Bond girl, and you lose a ball.*

Knowing better than to poke the bear, Julian gave her a mischievous grin. "Rihanna."

I'll take it. At least it's better than Pussy Galore.

"To Jimmy and Rihanna."

They all clinked glasses, and a small round of golf-clap responses filled the air.

Kathryn swallowed the brut and the need to plot her best friend's death, and let herself be dazzled by the brilliant piece of jewelry shining before her.

"That's quite the piece," she said, staring at it in disbelief.

Quite the piece wasn't the half of it. It was extraordinary. Her fingertips brushed the long single strand of stunning diamonds.

"Isn't it?" Anthony said proudly. "I know it's not the style of the piece Mr. Russo purchased, but it's the closest to the price range of the one he and his partner have."

"Partner?" Kathryn and Julian repeated in unison, giving each other a questioning glance before returning their surprised faces to Anthony.

He simply nodded.

Kathryn felt Julian press the strength of his palm to hers, tangling their fingers together. Losing all traces of an accent, he probed further.

"What gave you the impression they were more than friends?"

With certainty, Anthony raised a knowing brow. "I've been in this business long enough, I can tell the signs. The adorable banter. The loving looks. The way they seemed to know what each other thought before they said it. I'm a true romantic. It's why I work here. *J'adore l'amour.*"

Kathryn smartly translated the small phrase using her mostly forgotten high school French. *He loves . . . love? This can't be happening.*

"What did this partner look like?" she asked, trying not to snap at the salesclerk. Epic fail.

Anthony held his hand up so high. "About this tall. Espresso eyes. Raven hair. Gorgeous smile. And looking absolutely stunning walking out of here with that exquisite piece of jewelry."

The gnawing in the pit of Kathryn's gut turned biting and cold. She didn't have to guess who that was. Anthony's description said it all.

How could Jake do this? I saw the receipt. He purchased a necklace—worth more than a car—and not for his mother. Not for me. But for . . . Andi?

Kathryn made a feeble attempt at rational thought. Not easy, since every time she did, all she could see was Jake with Andi massaging his arm. And images of his ropes. Followed by herself going to town on said ropes with a tactical ax.

Could this be like Troy? A BDSM partner? Another sub?

Kathryn thought she and Jake were solid. Hell, he'd proposed.

But facts were facts.

This was what Kathryn did best. Research. Investigate. Wade through the bullshit to discover the truth.

The truth fucking sucks.

"More champagne?" Anthony asked.

I'm going to be sick.

Julian wrapped a consoling arm around her. "We're gonna need something stronger." He kissed her temple. "Let's go," he said, softly ushering her out the door.

The only way to deal with this was cold turkey. "I can't go to Jake's."

Julian patted her hand. "Say no more."

Kathryn didn't need to tell her best friend the drill. He knew.

Death by dessert. Mind-numbing amounts of hard liquor. She wasn't picky. Moonshine. Rotgut. Whatever would keep her from exploring her emotions or talking to Jake. Because talking led to crying—and that so wasn't happening. And talking led to getting the wool pulled over your eyes while he was shacking up with another sub.

Talking might also lead to murder.

Julian was a lot of things, but performing the duties of a grave digger would cause him to sweat. And everyone knew the man hated to sweat.

But her best friend was a girl's girl. He'd keep Kathryn from doing anything stupid. Because stupid, wasted drunk was calling her name.

And absolutely, positively no talking.

∾

Twelve hours and a half-dozen drinks later, Kathryn eyed the expensive bottle of bourbon in her hand. "And let me tell you something, Jake Russo . . . You, sir, are an ass."

This was some impressive top-shelf stuff Julian had splurged on. Whatever corner the man worked to buy this highbrow shit was totally worth it. She took another swig.

"I'm an ass?" Jake's words emanated calmly from the speaker of Julian's phone.

"You sure as hell are. And not because you have an ass—everybody knows you have an ass. A smoking-hot biscuit of an ass—"

"Hell yeah, he does," Julian shouted in support, a show of solidarity for who knew who at this point.

Kathryn wasn't the only one stupid wasted. She, however, was not naked. Or flaunting her wares out the luxury penthouse balcony at the great state of Colorado.

"Why don't I come get you?" Jake asked.

Wondering if it were two thirty in the morning or three thirty, Kathryn squinted in vain at the blurry clock.

"We can talk," he added.

"Talk?" That set her off. "There will be *nooo* talking," she screeched, full-throttle pissed off. "I," she pointed to herself with the bottle, "am not speaking to you, Sir Ass-a-lot."

"Can I speak with Julian?"

"Julian . . ." Kathryn checked out the balcony serving as a stage for her gyrating friend. "He's not talking to you either."

She tucked the bottle under her arm, devoting both hands to her phone.

Muttering, "Where's the FaceTime," she pressed a button. "Here. Julian," she hollered. "Jake wants to talk to you."

Loud, but not in the frame, Julian was heard shouting, "I am so gonna eat your ass, Ass Man."

Cocking his head, Jake lifted a stunned brow. Kathryn thought it over for a beat, shook her head, and translated. "He meant beat your ass."

Exasperated, Jake said, "It's Julian. Are you sure?"

With the camera pointed strategically, she pivoted her body, bringing Julian's birthday suit in full view of the phone. "Julian, tell Jake what you think of him?"

"Wooooo. Take that, Ass Man!" Julian cried with reckless abandon, smacking his ass for the world and the camera, that perfect triple threat of naked, stupid, and wasted.

Determined, she moved the screen to his butt.

Julian was all in, popping his SquatMaster-sculpted hiney right at the screen. "Uh, uh, uh. Take it, take it, take it!"

18

JAKE

I'm blind.

Jake's eyes slammed shut. Watching Julian prance around, shoving his ass at the screen and shouting, "Take it, take it, take it," was a bit much, even for him.

Never mind that it was nearly four in the morning, and he'd been up all night trying to figure out what the hell was going on. Whatever had Kathryn fired up wasn't exactly settling to a simmer.

No, Jake knew it was in everyone's best interest that they all get some sleep, then discuss it when calmer—and more sober—heads prevailed.

Pinching the bridge of his nose, he deadpanned, "I'm going to bed. Try to get some rest. And some water. I'll pick you up in a few hours."

"No dice, Ass Man. I'm not telling you where I am, and we have nothing to discuss. Go play with your other sub. The one you bought the necklace for. Yeah, I know about that. But do me a favor. When you tie her up, use different ropes."

The FaceTime call disconnected.

Jake stared at the phone, dazed and not exactly sure what the fuck just happened. But by now, it really didn't matter. He'd traced Kathryn's steps to the jewelers this afternoon—an *oh shit* moment he'd worry about later. Then he'd nearly lost her when she must have shut off the location services of her phone and taken Julian's car.

Thankfully, his credit-card alerts had lit up like a nuclear warning for an incoming missile.

After all, a pre-charge authorization was required for any purchase over ten thousand dollars. And charged on his black card that day, along with a penthouse suite and over the top orders of premium liquor, were Wagyu steaks and two one-thousand-dollar ice cream sundaes with gold leaf on them.

Jake had merely scratched his head before tapping the button. *Approved.*

It was a cutthroat move by Julian to punish him on Kathryn's behalf, but who could blame him? Kathryn was upset. Hell, Jake would be the first to splurge if it would draw her back from the high of a level-ten atomic freak-out.

But at least she wasn't crying. Instead, she was one riled-up kitten who thought Jake had a sub on the side. How the tires on every vehicle in the garage hadn't been slashed into playground mulch was beyond him.

And who could blame her in her conclusions, as ridiculous as they were. With his mysterious travels and the jewelry purchase—the one his wallet still wept softly over—it was easy to see how a kick-ass insurance investigator might come to that conclusion.

Jake didn't bother stifling his cheesy grin. If only she knew. He let out a full belly laugh at the thought of her face when she discovered "the other sub" was actually Paco.

Laughing when my kitten is frazzled. Wrong. Funny and just one more notch in a long line of reasons I'm going to hell.

But wrong.

19
JAKE

*J*ake tore away from his work when music hit the air. The light melodies of his new finder alert. With the melodic chimes of "Stray Cat Strut" playing, his kitten had to be on the move. In her own car.

He could only imagine the hangover Kathryn must have, and the pounding headache that was probably still lingering like a raging storm cloud over her head. If there was one thing his kitten needed to get through the day, it was a jolt of caffeine.

After stopping at Starbucks to order a tall dark Arabica for himself and a cappuccino with almond milk for her, Jake headed to phlebotomy class, the one place she was sure to show up that day, no matter how miffed she was. Her pattern was blissfully predictable.

Call Julian. Plan an escape route. And avoid Jake like a leper colony.

But regardless of the depth of her anger—or her hangover—under no circumstances would Nurse Chase bow out of her responsibilities. His girl might not have showered or brushed her teeth, but she would be at the class she was scheduled to teach, and she'd be there on time. Like a sniper, or stalker, all he had to do was hang out outside the classroom and wait.

"Jake?"

The cultured voice came from behind him, the man's alligator shoes clicking toward him from down the hall.

"Hey." Jake beamed a smile, motioning to the two hot coffees he held. Otherwise, he'd have manners enough to shake Carter's hand. "If it isn't the man who saved my life. I didn't realize you were back."

"Technically, Kathryn saved your life. She did the heavy lifting. The rest of us were more or less the cleanup crew." The man's brow quirked up. "I'm surprised she didn't mention seeing me."

"I've been in and out of town," Jake said with a shrug, playing it off because Kathryn hadn't said one word about bumping into Dr. Carter Reeves. Funny how *hey, Jake, I ran into my ex-husband* must have slipped her mind.

"It's great working with her again. And teaching phlebotomy is just the start. If she enjoys it, I intend to move her up the ladder pretty fast."

Jake took a long sip of his coffee, trying to get inside the mind of the woman he'd planned to marry, and understand why she hadn't said anything to him about this. "She's great at what she does," he muttered through clenched teeth.

"I'm just glad she wanted to teach this class. Between you and me, I'm surprised she accepted."

"So am I."

Jake wasn't usually the jealous type, and Kathryn was hardly his little woman, but to the explosive alpha in him, she sure as hell was. *His*. His woman. His kitten. His sub. In that order, with the operative word being *his*.

"I have to confess," Carter said with a sigh, "I've been trying to steal her away for dinner. I even told her it would be nothing fancy. I know how Kathryn hates the fancy stuff. Talk some sense into her, will you? Tell her she can't avoid her new boss forever."

Carter's two hearty pats on Jake's arm were a little too close to pushing him to the tipping point. It would be so easy to tear off the man's hand and feed it to him. Nothing fancy.

Jake sucked in a long breath before easing it out through his nose. "Dinner?"

"Oh." Carter's brows pinched in concern. "I know the two of you have a little thing going on, so I won't keep her the whole night. Just long enough to give her what she needs."

The man is dead. And what the fuck does he mean by "little thing"? Nothing, and I mean nothing in our relationship even comes close to the definition of "little."

Jake refrained from the third-grade move of whipping his dick out right then and there, although the thought crossed his mind. Before he could set the coffee cups down—just in case his juvenile impulses overtook him—Kathryn was joining them.

Jake always experienced a strange sense of pride as he watched Kathryn in her element. With or without scrubs, a stethoscope, or a mile-a-minute emergency-room tempo, Kathryn belonged in a hospital. It was who she was. That, coupled with the soft waves of her hair tickling her shoulders, should have earned her a kiss.

Unsettled to see her sunglasses high on her face, Jake studied her. Kathryn crying wasn't an option. When she finally took them off, the only redness in her eyes was from a massive bender and what he estimated to be about a whopping two hours of sleep.

She's fine. Game on.

It was easy to tell by the look on her face that she couldn't quite decide who to address first or who to stand next to. The arch of Jake's brow had her dropping her gaze to her feet.

"I brought you a coffee." Jake kept his voice calm, imagining the eerie still of the ocean in the moments before a tsunami.

"Thank you." Kathryn's voice was quiet and reserved as she avoided eye contact, though she held out her hand, ready to accept the cup.

But Jake didn't release it. There they stood, each of them awkwardly clinging to the cup.

Not until you face me, kitten.

As if she could read his thoughts, Kathryn gave in. She looked up, defiant and stubborn, and stared him down with her deep green eyes.

And then, like the last gusts of wind after a raging storm, the spark in her gaze faded. She let go.

Jake studied her, watching as she made a slow turn to the only other man standing there.

"I need to get started. Did you need me for something, Carter?"

Maybe it was the way she said his name, or the way she crossed her arms that lifted her breasts ever so slightly, or the way she just licked her lips, but his little girl was playing with fire.

And if fire is what she wants, an inferno is what she'll get.

"The usual," Carter said, without too much charm but just enough to be annoying as shit. "Checking in. Seeing how you're doing. Badgering you about dinner."

Jake refrained from killing him because the man had technically saved his life. But at this point, they were even.

"Dinner," Kathryn said, seeming to ponder the invitation as she slid a sidelong glance at Jake. "Dinner sounds great. Tonight. Text me."

"Perfect. I promise, I won't keep you long." Carter gave an infuriating wink to Jake, then moved on with his day.

Which left Kathryn in the uncomfortable position of having nothing between them to protect her. And at this point, she needed protection. If she for one second thought Jake had been hard on her in the past, her big bad Dom had only just begun.

Jake tossed the coffees in a nearby trash can and closed the distance between them in a single stride. But she looked a little too comfortable. His next step pushed her back against the wall, where she couldn't run, couldn't fight, and was forced to meet his eyes.

Towering over her, he spoke. "I know you have things on your mind. So do I. Don't think for two seconds I won't fuck you up against this wall to prove a point. But maybe we should start by talking."

With every one of her indecisive breaths, Jake was biding his time. Letting her breasts rise and fall against his body.

Dipping his head so she could feel the heat of his breath on her neck, he growled out, "I'm losing patience. Patient Jake was last night.

Today you have your Dom. And you have about thirty seconds to decide how this game will be played."

Kathryn swallowed hard. "We'll talk later."

He took half a step back, opening his arm and gesturing to the door. "After you."

Slowly, Kathryn made wary steps forward, then stopped in the doorway and turned around. "What are you doing? I agreed to talk later."

"What does it look like? I'm going to class."

Her eyes widened, the spark of something igniting behind them. It was a look Jake knew too well. It wasn't hunger. And it wasn't delight. It was rage. Kathryn's pure unadulterated rage was coming out and aimed at him in full force.

"No, you are not," she gritted out, her jaw tight.

Jake patted the nametag on his chest. "See this, Nurse Chase? This is my all-access pass. You wouldn't deprive an EMT from getting recertified, would you? Oh, look. A seat opened up right up front."

Grinning from ear to ear, Jake was pressing his luck, and he knew it. But poking the bear was part of his nature. It was Kathryn who had the taste for flight.

But he knew she wouldn't fly away this time. She was expected to be front and center in a room full of students, and as well as he knew himself, he knew she'd never back away from that. Jake was fully prepared for what awaited him. Kathryn would spend the next ninety minutes ignoring him completely when she wasn't shooting him death glares. He'd take them all in stride.

He had no issues coming out and telling her how all of this was a total misunderstanding. But let this serve as her punishment for trying to make him jealous with her ex. He couldn't imagine anything more punishment-worthy. But this would only be the start. There would be no satisfying either one of them until she was begging for forgiveness.

Well, forgiveness and my cock.

"Step aside, Nurse Chase." Jake wasn't harsh or aggressive when he said it. He lifted his lips in a half smile that double-dared her. The one that usually coaxed her out of anything.

Her brow relaxed, and her own smile mirrored his. This was the connection they shared.

Their tease of a stare-off was interrupted by a few late stragglers. Both Jake and Kathryn took a single step aside to let them pass. The low rumble of good afternoons was broken up by a sweet, "Hi, Kathryn," and a slightly sweeter, "Hi, Jake."

"Hey, Andi." Jake took a quick glance at his watch before returning his gaze to Kathryn. The glide of his hand smoothed across her arm naturally. His voice was tender and coaxing. "We should probably get inside, Teach."

Kathryn's smile dropped and her entire demeanor changed. But her feet didn't budge. Instead, she let the word slip from her lips. A single word that once said, was out there. There was no arguing. No reasoning. It had the power of an ice-cold bucket of pure holy water against a vampire mid-attack.

Wearily, she said, "Red."

There was nothing left for Jake to do. People always think it's the Dom who has all the power, but they're wrong. It's the sub. Jake knew the expectation. He was to hold his tongue and back away.

But if ever the circumstances called for him to break the rules, this was it. He didn't break them often, but walking away from Kathryn Chase like this? Not on his life. Without thinking, he pulled the classroom door closed to avoid prying eyes from within, raised both arms along the frame, and towered over her as he caged her in.

Her eyes widened, and it was apparent she hadn't been expecting that. At all.

Silent, Kathryn lifted a defiant chin, followed by curving her lush lips in an equally defiant pout.

Jake could see what she was doing. His lips ticked up not so much in a smile, but in mild exasperation. The clock was ticking. He had exactly half a second to step away or risk a knee to the balls.

His forehead lowered to hers. Her breathing was ragged and stifled, then not there at all.

For once, he wasn't going to remind her to breathe. She would do plenty of that once he left. He wasn't going to reason with her, or ask. Or beg.

When will she learn? She can run all she wants, but I'll never be too far away.

Jake leaned to the side, and his soft words feathered over her ear. "This isn't over."

20

KATHRYN

Kathryn had the key to escape the hot prison walls of Jake Russo. She always did. The key to walk away from the endless warmth of his eyes, the magnetic draw of his solid build, the tender trap of his touch. A key that would free her—if only for the moment. But a moment was what she needed. To be free.

From him.

"Red," she said so softly she wasn't sure he heard it. But by the look in his eyes, he did.

The fire that always blazed bright for her behind those hazel eyes dimmed. The closeness between them cooled. But his hand stayed wrapped around her arm, holding her in place as his forehead lowered to hers. Every word he spoke rumbled through her, stirring every piece of her existence to heed him.

"This isn't over. Listen very carefully, little kitten. I'll stop for the moment because you have that power. You always have and you always will. But make no mistake, I might be releasing you, but I'm not letting you go. You're mine."

Jake slipped an arm past her, barely touching her side as he opened the door. It was enough for her to take a needed step back.

Why did the emptiness between them feel colder in that moment?

She could have said she wanted to talk. Agreed to meet with him later. But she wasn't about to, and he knew that. He knew it and did what he always did . . . insisted on not letting her go.

In an instant, his hand unlocked its grip around her arm, giving her everything she asked for and nothing she wanted. The freedom to walk away.

Already half regretting her short steps away, she hurried, desperate to put more distance between them. To breathe.

Breathing was hard enough when Jake's body was pressed up against her, but with him gone, her chest tightened until she felt like she was suffocating. Slowly, Kathryn became aware of the low murmurs of the class, the uncomfortable rustling of students eager to get started.

She untwisted the knots inside herself and with each step, fought her way through the quicksand of emotions holding her back, eventually making her way behind the lectern. Glancing at the open doorway, she discovered Jake had gone.

Over the next hour, Kathryn broke up her boring-as-shit lectures with several exercises that would give the students just the type of hands-on learning they craved. For the most part, these were nurses —*my people*—each with their own calling to do more for others than they did for themselves.

Even the dark-haired beauty in the back. Other than Jake, Andi was the only other student who wasn't a nurse.

For the love of God, why does she have to be so sweet? Look at her. Without a partner, quietly watching others, practicing on her own goddamn arm.

"Let me help," Kathryn said before she could stop herself.

"Thanks. The angle was a little hard like this."

Kathryn swept away Andi's guilt and offered her own arm. "It is," she said, remembering. It was how she'd practiced.

Back then, everyone practiced on patients. It never seemed right.

How were nurses supposed to learn if they didn't understand that the slightest shift in angle and pressure made all the difference?

Knowing what you were doing made you confident. Made you a better nurse. Maybe made you a better sub.

Just as Jake had, Kathryn yelped with the initial prick of the sharp point of the needle. Andi froze. "That's it," Kathryn said, reassuring her. "You're doing fine."

The relief on Andi's face was apparent, her lips lifting to an unsure smile as her stress melted away. "I'm sorry you have to get stuck with me. Literally. I didn't realize Jake couldn't make class."

"Yeah, he, uh, couldn't stay."

It was easy to see why Andi would make the perfect sub. She was warm. Attentive. Took to the details. Was more than eager to please. It was like some part of her was naturally inclined to serve. Craving it, even. And that was the reason why she'd make the perfect nurse, though she wasn't. Add to that she had legs going on for days, and a slender body that probably wouldn't quit.

"I don't get much practice at the pharmacy," Andi said.

"Mostly vaccines?" Kathryn asked.

Andi nodded, concentrating. Kathryn kept an eye on her work. Watching Andi fill a single vial, undo the tourniquet, remove the needle, and smile.

Her big dark eyes looked at Kathryn with childlike eagerness. "How'd I do?"

"Well . . ." Kathryn sighed, looking for even the tiniest excuse to find a flaw in what had been done. But she couldn't. "You did well."

A rush of air whooshed from Andi's lips. "Oh, good." With both her hands, she held her heart. "I was so nervous. Worried I'd let you down."

Oh, for Christ's sake.

"Class is over for today," Kathryn announced, so ready for this to be over. "You all did great. See you back here on Tuesday."

With a painfully wide smile that showed every last one of her teeth, Andi smoothed a hand over Kathryn's.

"I have a feeling we'll see each other before Tuesday." Andi leaned her Vegas showgirl body in, whispering, "Saturday. Club Lazarus. I have a collar with your name on it."

"You . . . have a collar for me?"

"Mm-hmm. I don't want to spoil the surprise, but maybe you should wear something red. I'll bet you look great in red."

If Andi was trying to be sweet, she'd succeeded. Overly so. Like when you sprinkle a little extra stevia in your tea. No matter how much you convince yourself it's fine, it just ends up leaving the wrong taste in your mouth.

Not unlike this. And the rushed side hug before Andi raced out of the room made it all the more awkward.

Watching her leave, Kathryn sighed.

She loved Jake. She did. Truly loved him with all her heart. And there might have been a chance he could have kept her and had a sub on the side.

Like, if he kept me as his prisoner. Or when hell froze over.

Because there was no way on God's green earth that was happening. His chances of being struck by lightning while simultaneously winning the lottery and bowling a strike were a trillion times greater.

And not just because she wasn't into polygamy, which she wasn't. Or free expression. Which she completely was. But the thought of a sub on the side ranked up there with menthol cigarettes, six-inch heels, or Brazilian wax jobs. Great for some people, just not for her.

Kathryn grabbed her purse and fished the preference sheet from it, along with a pen.

So I carry the preference sheet with me? Don't judge. I might find a random type of kink that interests me. And if I don't write it down when I'm thinking of it, I'll forget.

When she got to the part of the list that asked about multiple partners, she thought long and hard for almost a second. With a big fat check, she filled in the only box that made sense for her.

Hard. Limit.

21

JAKE

"Julian. Open up."

Pounding louder than before, Jake also used the hotel suite's doorbell. If Julian's late checkout had anything to do with what was undoubtedly a hangover of epic proportions, noise was truly the Antichrist. "Come on, Julian, open the door."

Julian finally did, but only a crack. "Jake," he said, scanning his visitor up and down from behind the wall of his door. "I'm a little busy now. Come back for therapy about your woes with Kathryn another time."

"Not a chance."

"Talk it out with Kathryn. This is between you and her." Indignant, Julian shut the door. His then engaging both the chain lock and the deadbolt were totally unnecessary.

Unamused, Jake wasn't going to break the door down, though it crossed his mind. And he wasn't about to scream through it like a drama queen. That was Julian's job.

Instead, he lowered his voice. "You've got thirty seconds to let me in before I call the bank and claim my credit card was stolen."

"You wouldn't," came muffled through the door.

Jake tugged out his phone and held it up to the peephole. "I'm calling now," he said loudly, driving the point home with sadistic satisfaction.

"All right, all right," Julian said through the door as he unlocked and cracked it open again. With a resigned huff, he mumbled, "Just . . . don't judge."

"Never," Jake said, which might be a lie. After all, this was Julian. Hell, anything could be waiting for him behind that door.

Patiently waiting for the door to open enough he could step through, Jake pocketed his phone in the back of his jeans and repeated the words over and over in his head.

Don't judge. Don't judge. Don't. Judge.

The door did eventually open enough so Jake could enter, but barely. Inside, Julian stood, shirtless and in a pair of jeans that couldn't possibly be his. From the twisted angst on his face and each staggered huff, the waistband of the jeans had to be cutting off his circulation as well as his breathing.

Not sure he actually wanted the answer, Jake winced and asked the question with dread. "Are those Kathryn's jeans?"

"You said you wouldn't judge," Julian snapped.

"I'm not judging." Total lie. "Just asking a question."

The words tumbled out at full speed. "I was only trying them on for a second to see if they would fit. Which they do."

Jake snorted. "Obviously."

"And then the zipper got stuck. I've worked this zipper harder than a hand around Ryan Gosling's dick, but it's no use. It's locked in place like an alligator nipple clamp."

Seeing Julian squeezed into Kathryn's favorite jeans, Jake understood Julian's predicament. "So, Kathryn might have let you live for trying on her jeans, but she'll straight-up shank you if you do so much as look at them crossways with a pair of shears."

"Exactly." Julian huffed out several exaggerated breaths, then sucked in his gut. "Jake, this is a matter of life or limb. I can barely wiggle my toes." He pressed his palms together in desperate prayer. "I know you have a switchblade somewhere on you, because you're just the sort of rugged lumberjack that would. I'm begging you. Do your worst and set me free from this ungodly banana trap of a torture device."

Smirking, Jake pulled the knife in question from his boot and flicked open the blade, lightly rubbing the scruff on his cheek with it, narrowing his eyes. "So, it's okay if Kathryn murders me?"

"We both know you're a dead man walking anyway."

Death glares exchanged, Jake left the room, and Julian nearly had a heart attack.

"I can't believe you're leaving me, you heartless bastard!"

Jake returned from the bathroom, holding up a small bar of soap. "Heartless bastard?"

"I mean, thank you for not abandoning me in my time of need. You're a saint." Julian batted his eyes before grabbing the soap. With a look that clearly telegraphed *you poor man*, he pointed the soap at him. "This is where being a lumberjack is your downfall. If anything was gonna slick these pants off, it would be lube. But since I came here with Kathryn, I failed to adequately prepare."

"It's for the zipper. Bar soap is tried and true for releasing the teeth. Rub it on the zipper and pull."

"Rub and pull. It's like I was born ready."

Eager to avoid watching Julian's hand job, Jake made himself busy around the room.

"While you're wandering around," Julian called out, "see if you can find Kathryn's phone."

"Shouldn't be difficult." Jake spoke into his watch. "Locate kitten. Sound alarm."

A muffled rendition of "Bad Girls" by Donna Summer was coming from the couch. Jake moved two pillows aside. Tucked in the corner of the sofa was Kathryn's phone. Next to her engagement ring. As he picked it up, he heard a loud *zzzip*.

"Oh, thank God. I can breathe again. You're a lifesaver. You and your amazing hacks for soap. What other penitentiary tricks do you have rolled up in those impressive sleeves?"

Jake didn't turn to face him. He hardened his gaze, staring at the small piece of jewelry that represented his whole heart.

Julian stepped up next to him, his sharp gasp revealing he was as surprised to see the ring as Jake was. But instead of being compassionate or understanding, Julian snapped at him.

"Well, what do you expect?" Julian said, and when Jake scowled at him, he did the unthinkable, fiercely poking Jake straight in the chest. "*You* have been two-timing my best friend. And as grateful as I am for the use of your black card and the soap that unlocked my dick from that denim cock-cage, that is not okay. You hear me, Jake Russo? Not. Okay."

"I would never cheat on Kathryn."

"Well, I've already confirmed you're not in a thruple, so why else would you buy an outrageous piece of jewelry for Andi?"

Jake jerked his head back. "Andi? I haven't so much as bought that woman a stick of gum. Why would Kathryn think I bought anything for Andi?"

"Because the salesclerk at Hayes said you did."

Julian was speaking, but the words weren't registering.

Jake frowned at him. "Anthony said I bought jewelry for Andi?"

Nodding, Julian crossed his arms and tapped one foot, certain of himself. "He said you were with your partner, and described Andi to a T. Exhaustively descriptive about her *espresso eyes* and *raven hair*. Who even talks like that? Oh, and a gorgeous smile that only pales in comparison to the fucking necklace she apparently walked out of the store with." Ending with a huff, Julian had made his point.

"First of all, the person sure as hell wasn't my partner . . . well, not in that way. And what about the girl who abandoned her engagement ring? Flirted with her ex in front of me? Arranged to have dinner with him?"

"She's having dinner with Carter Reeves? Wow . . . torturing herself to lash out at you. It's like I've taught her nothing." Julian slumped to the sofa. "None of this would have happened if you hadn't been a d-bag."

"I'm not a d-bag. The jewelry was for Kathryn." Jake sat beside him, losing himself in the twinkle of the diamonds in the ring.

"Then why give it to Andi?"

"Oh, for the love of God, Julian. I was with Paco. Not Andi."

"Paco?" Julian asked. "As in Paco Robles?"

Jake nodded as he slid the ring between the first and second knuckle of his pinky.

Sitting up and attentive, Julian leaned in. "So, Paco Robles . . . exists? All this time, I was pretty sure Kathryn made him up. From what she's described, he's a smoking-hot unicorn. I figured Paco was code for"— he curled his fingers in air quotes—"*I need some me time*. I mean, come on. Kathryn has two fabulous gay friends? Two fabulous gay friends who have never met each other? Inconceivable," he said, mimicking Vizzini from *The Princess Bride*.

Jake looked over, the *I don't know what to tell you, man* look blaring through. "Paco Robles is very much real. And believe it or not, Anthony described him perfectly. Espresso eyes. Raven hair. Gorgeous smile, although I'm not sure I would've used those exact words to describe him. That's what makes it funny."

"I guess it would be funny . . . if it hadn't marked you for murder. Look," Julian patted his hand, "your secret is safe with me."

Between the extra-long pat on his hand and the questionable look of understanding in Julian's eyes, Jake was almost afraid to ask. "And what secret would that be?"

"Obviously, you're having an affair with that hot stud Robles."

Oh my God. This is how rumors start.

"Julian—"

"Hey, I get it. From how Kathryn carries on about him, I'm too impressed to be upset. And if you need to butter both sides of your biscuit, seriously, no judgment. I mean, from what I can tell, the man seems a little out of your league . . ."

Jake struggled not to react to the dig. *Nice.*

"But you should really tell Kathryn."

Jake dropped his head to his hand, huffing out an exasperated breath. "There is nothing to tell."

"Hang on. Didn't Kathryn once ask him to be her Dom?"

Jeez, she really does tell him everything.

It took a second before Jake shrugged, admitting what Julian obviously already knew.

"So, how is Daddy Jake hitting it with a fellow Dom?"

With a sound that can only be described as a wounded battle cry, guttural and frustrated, Jake stood up. "I'm leaving now."

"Not without me, you're not. You can't leave me hanging. It's like getting to the last few pages of the steamy male-female-male romance novel, where some heartless bastard has ripped the pages from the binding."

"So, I'm back to being a heartless bastard?"

"Not if you wait up."

22

KATHRYN

"So, this is where you work?" Paco asked, letting Kathryn lead as they strolled down the long hall.

After having visited with the detective and Troy in their room, Kathryn offered to walk Paco out of the hospital. Which would have been faster if she knew exactly where she was going. She'd only been a few places in that hospital, and with Troy being moved to another room again, losing her bearings was easy. But she knew the general direction of the exit, and if she didn't eventually figure the way out, she could always ask for directions since there was a nurses' station about every twelve rooms.

Kathryn let out a long sigh. "Can I ask you something?"

"The last time you asked me that, you asked me to be your Dom."

She smiled at the warmth of that memory. "I'm needy that way."

Paco's muscular shoulder nudged hers, before he winged out an arm. "Shoot. What's on your overanalytical mind?"

Sliding her arm around his, she asked, "Is it common in the lifestyle? Being with more than one partner?"

"As the risk of sounding repetitive, this is probably something you should be discussing with Jake. The truth of the matter is that nothing is common in the lifestyle. Are you thinking about," he paused, "branching out?"

"No, not me." *How can he ask me that?* "It's Jake."

"Jake?"

"There's this other woman—"

"Stop." Paco took a cautious step back, dipping his head and meeting her eyes. He kept his voice as low, taking into considering they were in a very public place. "You know I'm a vault. And I will always be here for you. As uncomfortable as it makes me to ask this, and just so you and I are crystal clear, are you saying Jake wants to see you with another woman?"

"What? No. I mean . . . I don't know. Oh my God, I didn't even think of that. Andi said she wanted to connect this weekend. What if that's the surprise? The gift that keeps on giving. A sub . . . for his sub?"

After a minute of nothing but a squeak emanating from her parted lips, and Paco's patient eyes smiling down on her, Kathryn answered her own question, making the words sound more like a question than a statement.

"No . . ." She let the word settle for a second, saying more firmly, "No. I don't think so."

"Let's start over." Paco began strolling, settling her hand into the crook of his arm that was always there to pull her along. "You have a question."

Kathryn's light giggle was quickly quashed as she saw Carter at the end of the hall. He was running, and the man never ran. Not unless there was an emergency.

Her arm dropped from Paco's. Understanding, he stepped back, giving them room.

"What's going on? Can I help?" she asked, racing alongside Carter. They'd spent too many years in the field together. The give and take, needs and expectations, they become instinctual.

"Yes. Smart of me to have you already credentialed at this hospital. We're needed in the ER. A major pileup on the freeway ended in a gas-tanker explosion. Three buses of grade schoolers en route to a choir competition were among the injured. They're diverting everyone to several hospitals, and we're the closest. You're not completely cleared and can't assist in surgery, but we could use your help."

Damn insurance rules.

Kathryn turned back, ready to apologize profusely for abandoning her friend. But Paco was gone.

Keeping up with Carter as she picked up the pace, she said, "You've got it."

23
KATHRYN

"*Kathryn?*"

Despite the tenderness of the man's voice, her name snapped through the air like an electrical charge. Kathryn and Carter both startled and turned around.

"Jake." Kathryn breathed out his name, not ready to see him.

Not ready to see his dark eyes look down at her as he asked what was wrong. Not ready to admit to either him or herself that she wasn't ready for this part of his life. She couldn't deal with sharing him, not having all of him to herself. She needed the most authentic part of Jake Russo to be hers and hers alone, and she needed to be his.

"How did you—"

But he only glanced at her for a second. Eye to eye with Carter, he asked, "What can we do?"

Julian raced up beside him. "You've got a lot incoming, Doc. I'm guessing we can be of service."

Carter glanced between the two of them and quickly sized them up. "Are you medically trained and vetted with this hospital?"

Julian nodded. "I am. I'm an RN."

"EMT," Jake said. "I won't be able to assist you in surgery, but I can triage out here."

Carter's skilled hands landed on both Jake and Julian's shoulders. "Consider yourselves deputized. Kathryn, grab them some badges so everyone knows they're legit."

"Right away." Hurrying, she raced to the manager, explaining the situation and requesting lanyards with visiting medical team credentials.

In a sharp turn back, she'd landed herself front and center before a wall of Jake, his solid body blocking hers. Between the hard lines of his face and the heat of his towering body, she couldn't move.

"Kathryn—"

His single determined step erased the distance between them, but still, she held her walls high. As high as she could. But her armor was so flimsy and paper thin, if he touched her, she'd crumple.

"We need to talk." Deliberate, his tone deepened to a point that halted her defiant steps, holding her in place with nothing more than the heat of his body and the strength of his will against her weak resolve. Because this was the man she was bound to . . . a man who had all her heart. Even if part of it was shredded and barely functioning right now.

"This isn't the time."

"No, it's not," he said. It wasn't a command, but her body stilled as if it were. "But we're about to take on a wave of who knows what. A few broken bones or an onslaught of battered bodies. People who might be doing all they can just to hang on. To survive. And all I can think of is you."

His grip slipped around her arm. Not tightly, but it was there. Jake owned her. This man had a claim on her heart and always managed to capture it, no matter how many shattered pieces he ended up holding.

I've said it before and I can say it again. It would be so easy. Red. Just push it from my lips, step back, and walk away.

Without warning, his lips crashed onto hers.

Kathryn let the smoldering heat of his mouth warm hers because she wanted it. Wanted to forget everything but his hand sliding around to the small of her back. Move her palms up the broad shoulders she could never wrap her arms around without tiptoeing, and steal this moment. Forget whatever tension was between them and savor every long stroke of his tongue, every nibble along her mouth, and every breath of one good long kiss.

It was as if nothing had happened. This was Jake, and he always had a way of making her feel so damn good. The world was about to collapse around them, and this was the only truth.

And it was true. Jake loved her. And she only loved him.

Pushing away would be easy. This was hard, knowing they only had seconds before life happened in all the worst ways. But she could hang on to this. To him. For a few more precious seconds of saying everything and nothing at all.

When his lips moved away, he took her hand and slid something on her finger. "You're the only woman in my life, kitten."

He found it. My engagement ring. "But how—"

Sirens blared, starting in the distance but rushing in closer, approaching fast.

Julian cut in between them, looping lanyards over each of their heads and letting them slip around their necks. "I hope you two sorted out what you needed to, 'cause we've got incoming."

Jake's long fingers drifted along the back of her hand. She latched on, weaving her slender fingers through his and squeezing hard. The steadfast look in his eyes was one she returned.

This was what they'd both been trained for. *Patients first.*

His hand curled around the back of her neck as he pulled her close to exchange one last heartfelt kiss.

24
JAKE

"You're gonna be just fine," Jake said to the young boy while splinting his arm.

This one was lucky. A bad sprain, most likely, but only a radiologist in imaging would know for sure. The splint would keep the youngster from jostling his arm and doing any more damage in the interim.

For the most part, this was Jake's life. Or at least it was on every other Friday from six in the evening until around six in the morning.

But these weren't his normal patients. Partying college students. Domestic disputes. Drunks who'd slip and fall, or lash out and fight. Those were the garden-variety cases his services usually rewarded him with during his volunteer shifts.

But seeing this many children in one night? Each one was its own kick to the gut.

"Hang in there. A doctor will see you soon." Jake did his best, reassuring the boy with a hand on his shoulder. At least these kids' parents and guardians were here.

"Were you in combat?"

Jake's smile warmed. "I was. What gave it away?"

"Your killer tattoos," the boy said, staring wide-eyed at the few that were exposed on Jake's arm. The boy's gaze drifted to Jake's neck. "Was that from a bullet?"

Jake's hand moved to the long-forgotten wound, and he nodded. "What's your name?"

"Travis."

"Jake."

Dramatically, Travis widened his gaze and looked up. "Did you almost die?"

Jake shifted uncomfortably with the hero worship. Under his breath, he said, "Twice, actually."

Scanning across the busy waiting room, he had to find Kathryn. Had to at least see her in that moment.

"I'm gonna be a soldier one day, Mr. Jake." The boy beamed with pride, addressing Jake formally as his grade-school training kicked in.

Travis's father patted the boy's shoulder in a show of affection and pride, and Jake noticed similar tattoos on the man. After all, this was Colorado Springs, a city that was overflowing with military veterans.

Connected in pride, Jake forced a grin. It could be the endless hours on his feet, or maybe he was just getting old. But whatever he was feeling, it tugged at just enough angst that he was already worried for the eight-year-old.

"You'll make a hell of a fine one," Jake said, mustering a smile. "Just remember two things. First, look out for one another. Watch each other's backs. And second . . ."

Jake managed to catch a glimpse of Kathryn as his rushed little kitten took charge and kicked ass in the middle of the chaos. *Fuck, she's mind-blowing.*

It was a moment. Barely a second when in the midst of rushing and directing and holding it together, she stopped just long enough to sweep those thick strawberry-blonde waves into a ponytail high on her head. Her back arched in a fluid move, and his gaze followed down the lines of her body—tracing those curves that dipped at her waist and flared at her hips. A perfect breathtaking moment of nothing but Kathryn Chase.

"Second," Jake said, returning his attention to the boy, "be extra good to your nurse."

The young boy seemed equally infatuated with Kathryn as she glided from one bay to the next. He looked up at Jake, grinning wide. "Sir, yes, sir."

Jake kept up the pace for several more hours, and each time he ended with one patient, he was on to the next. Even tired and fatigued, nothing would keep him from helping every last person he could. Not unless he was ordered to stop. Or he passed out.

Dismayed, he huffed under his breath and rubbed his brow. "Shit. When will it end?"

"Here," Julian said, offering him his choice of Coke or Red Bull.

"Thanks." Jake grabbed the Coke, appreciating Julian more than he could know, with full understanding that the man lived for Red Bull.

"Oh, thank God. I was just being polite."

Jake cracked a smile. "I know," he said, popping open the can. The fizz and flavor were just the jolt he needed. "Ahh," he said, springing back to life. "Kathryn might need—"

"Already taken care of, big guy. Thanks, by the way, for the pizza in the lounge."

"My name shouldn't have been on the order. How did you know it was me?"

"Well, when I called as Jake Russo and tried to use your card, Francesco said that you'd already placed an order. Color me awkward. If you talk to him again soon, he might ask about your memory issues. Damn football injury."

"Speaking of my credit card . . ."

Julian's face fell, unusually guilt-ridden. "Fine."

He huffed, ditching his empty can in the recycling bin and opening his wallet. Holding it high between two fingers, he frowned.

"Here you go." True lament filled his words, and it was clear to both of them that that card wasn't leaving his hand unless Jake pried each finger off it.

"Keep it."

"Really?"

The extra pop of Julian's glee was enough for Jake to clarify. "Hey, I don't see my ring on your finger. Not forever, just for tonight."

"Why do men always say that to me?"

Jake glanced away, noticing a little girl who sat tucked away in the far corner of the room. *How did I miss her?* Balled up in her chair with her knees to her chin, the girl's angst-filled face and worried frown were too much to ignore.

Time to get back to work.

"Use that card," he told Julian. "Take care of anything that you think needs taken care of, and thanks for the drink."

Before he hurried off, Julian pressed a palm to his arm. "Kathryn was frantic, you know?"

He didn't know. Frantic? The little girl could wait thirty seconds more. He had to give Julian his full attention.

Concerned, he asked, "About what?"

"About the ring. She didn't take it off on purpose. Not like that. We went a little crazy with the appetizers, and at some point the guacamole might have tipped on her hand. Accidentally."

Jake smirked.

"She might have been accidentally trying to fish a corner of a chip out of it."

"That's my girl. No chip left behind."

"But you didn't hear it from me. Anyway, she washed her hands and scrubbed the hell out of that ring with her toothbrush—even handed it to me to show me the great job she did—and then I must have laid it down. Kathryn turned that hotel room upside down this morning, hung over and swearing at herself the whole time. Offered an obscene amount of money to housekeeping if they found it."

Jake's tight lips lifted in relief. "Thanks, Julian. I assume you've got video footage of my girl manhandling the guac?"

That warranted a chuckle. "Sending now."

A few more patients later, and Jake was ready for a bona fide break.

Just ten solid minutes to check up on his kitten before another few hours of work.

Kathryn wasn't hard to find. With the way her body zipped through the halls, it was as if she was everywhere at once. He caught up to her in a nearby room.

"It'll only sting for a second, but you'll start to feel much better." Quietly, she explained the procedure to the terrified wailing girl, her weeping mother, and an anxious young nurse. "Like this," she said, working through the steps of administering what could be a cortisone injection, or possibly a nerve block. Having a nurse like Kathryn administer the shot was rare enough. More unusual was for her to have to do it on a patient so young.

Loud voices echoing through the halls halted Kathryn mid-shot. Looking up, her eyes locked onto his. Her tight lips warmed with barely the trace of a smile. She lifted a brow, a silent plea as she narrowed her gaze deliberately at the door.

It was a delicate procedure. A momentary pause or a sudden move could go terribly wrong. They needed quiet. Privacy. And Jake had done what he'd come to do. Marginally, at best, he'd accomplished his small gesture to let her know he was thinking of her. Wanting to do more would have to wait. His short-lived presence would have to be enough.

Nodding in understanding, Jake smiled back and prepared to step out. The procedure shouldn't take long, but they needed to work. And the second his feet hit the hall, he'd be up to his collar in the next round of patients.

"Just the door, Mr. Russo. We could use your help."

Jake shut the door. "Yes, Nurse."

Yup. That made my dick twitch. She's in the middle of administering an excruciatingly painful injection, and I want to take her up against a wall. Reason I'm going to hell number two.

"Where do you want me?" he asked, and her sudden blush had *down, boy* written all over it.

"On the other side of us," she said.

Jake took his position, his trained smile emerging as he looked down on the hysterical little girl. Her mother tried holding her in place, but it was the point at which loved ones often failed. Not applying enough constraint. This close, the bulge in the child's knee was alarming.

She can't move.

Kathryn slipped into medical speak, hurried in her recap to catch him up. "Six-year-old admitted with a swollen knee. Fluid buildup below the kneecap. Possible meniscus tear. IV pain relievers administered with no effect. Pain is eased in this position," she indicated the pillow postured under the little girl's knee, "but barely."

She paused, apparently using code to avoid saying the words *surgery* or *operating room* in front of the small child. "Imaging ASAP—OR in two hours or less." She held up the shot. "Lidocaine to ease the immediate pain."

Numbing the pain would also keep the child from moving. If they were doing an X-ray or MRI, she'd have to refrain from any movements at all. Damn near impossible when you were in agony.

"Hold her still?" Jake asked.

"Please," Kathryn said calmly and directly.

Jake was gentle but firm as he directed the mother to the head of the bed. He needed her out of the way, but he knew mama bears. Based on the streams of tears sliding down her puffy cheeks, there was no way this woman would move more than two feet from her daughter's side.

"If you could hold her hand," he said. "Nurse Chase is the best. It'll only take a second."

It broke his heart to see the cute little girl with missing front teeth bawling her eyes out. But he knew the drill. No sedation. It was imperative that through most of this, they could ask her questions and she could answer.

No more talking was required. He and Kathryn didn't need to speak. They'd never worked together, but it was as if they'd worked together for years. Knew each other's glances. Read each other's thoughts.

Jake readied his hands, getting into position. Studying her eyes, he postured and waited.

The shift in Kathryn's features was subtle. Almost imperceptible. Her eyes dilated. The thumping pulse in her neck quickened, and her lips parted. Before she nodded or said *now*, his hands locked around the little girl's leg.

Needle in. Needle out. Hands eased off. It was over.

"There." Kathryn's shoulders relaxed and her tension dissipated. She expelled a small breath. Looking at the mom, she grinned. "In two minutes, she should start feeling a whole lot better."

And just like that, the deafening wailing stopped. Sniffling, the little girl raised her tear-filled eyes to Jake. "Thank you."

Embarrassed, Jake pocketed his hands, ready to shyly explain he'd done very little except hold her tiny little leg down.

"Yes." Kathryn gave him her warmest grin. "Thank you. You have the magic touch."

Jake made his way out of the room and waited, leaning on the wall just outside the door. It only took Kathryn a few more minutes to wrap up, and the second she stepped into the hall, their eyes met.

"I'll catch up with you in a bit, Megan," she said to the nurse.

"You were amazing in there." Jake didn't hold back his adoration. "That's a tough technique. Even harder when you're performing on a tiny knee like that, all while teaching."

"It's Megan's first night. She just graduated. The most she saw in her internship was a sprained wrist. She's doing great, but had no idea how to really handle an injection with a thirty-gauge needle. I probably should have let her do it, but—"

Jake couldn't help it. He jerked Kathryn into him, locking one arm around her waist as he cupped that damn gorgeous face in his other hand. "Using that little girl as a pincushion turned my stomach too. You did the right thing. You always do the right thing. I'm living proof."

Modest as ever, Kathryn turned her shy glance away, biting back a smile. It gave him the excuse he needed to lower the hand that was cupping her cheek to glide along her neck. His mild, soothing massage was welcomed. Her moan was almost inaudible. *Almost.*

"Do you need anything?"

Not now, she glared.

He chuckled in her ear. "Like food," he murmured, letting his hand drift further down her arm, brush her tummy, until two fingers slipped into the waistband of her jeans.

Her head shake was unhurried and indecisive. She could take all night contemplating whether or not she needed food. At least she wasn't pulling back or resisting.

"It'll just slow me down," she finally said, her big eyes meeting his. Leaning forward, she pressed against him. An attempt to get a better look at the waiting room, but he'd take it. It was the closest she'd felt to him in over a day.

Jake inhaled. Half a day on her feet, and he could still detect the fragrant notes of vanilla, a scent that always perfectly swirled with that singular smell of her.

"I figure two more hours at the most. I can hold out."

"Hmm?" *Hold out? Right. Food. She means food.*

"Late dinner?" He upped the ante. "And a massage?"

Maybe she was too tired to argue. Or maybe the idea felt just as right to her. Whatever the reason, she agreed. "Yes."

There was a long pause afterward. Her tongue made a gentle swipe along the fullness of her lower lip, in every way but physical driving him to his knees. Her big eyes searched his, eager to find something.

What?

He let his fingers slide along the velvety skin beneath her waistband. "Talk to me. What's on your mind."

"I—" She sucked in a breath. "I know what the surprise is."

"You do?"

It didn't take a rocket scientist to put two and two together to know how she figured it out. *Julian*. But for a woman about to receive more diamonds than South Africa, she didn't look particularly pleased. It was extravagant. Maybe she was worried about the cost.

"It's just a gift," he said, reassuring her with a peck. "But if you don't like it, we can always try something else. Hell, get a bunch and rotate them."

Jake couldn't be certain, but with her eyebrows shooting clear to her forehead . . . *is that fear?*

"I, uh . . ." The smallest gasp escaped from her throat before Kathryn whooshed out of breath. "I love you, Jake. And I trust you." Her words along with that sweet simmering gaze lit him in instant heat, until she said, "I'll try anything . . . once."

The *once* managed to resonate in the air, hanging between them with intense, strange energy.

Jake cocked his head. Twisting a woman's arm to be allowed to drape her in diamonds? It was the new definition of insanity.

Am I missing something?

"Here." She pressed a folded sheet of paper in his hands.

"What's this?"

"Nurse Chase?" Megan was up to her elbows, desperately searching for something in a trauma cart.

Kathryn popped up on her tiptoes to give him a small kiss. "Read it for yourself." Tearing herself away, she said, "Coming."

25
JAKE

I know I shouldn't read it now.

But the whole world of Kathryn Chase's most intimate fantasies and desires was in the palm of his hand. How could he fucking not?

As soon as he unfolded the first flap, he heard the cry.

"Waaaahhhhh!"

That would be little Tameka. The terrified girl who was balled up in a corner, too afraid to speak up and let anyone, including her mother, know exactly how much pain she was in. Turned out she'd been cradling a broken finger.

Crap.

Refolding the page and slipping it into his back pocket, his fingers brushed the top of Kathryn's phone. How the woman had managed to keep going this long without it was beyond him. *Take my phone, and I think my heart would stop.*

No point fussing over it now. He made peace with the technology now burning a hole in his pocket and double-timed it in the direction of the screams. He couldn't do much if they were realigning the bones in prep for splinting, but he could be there for Tameka. Smile, and let her know it would be all right.

Nearly three hours later, the waiting room was silent, the seats all empty except the one Jake was slumped in.

If his once-a-week EMT work had taught him anything, it was that peace was a fleeting concept that never lasted long. This was just the lull before the next storm. But at least for now, it meant Jake's work for the night was finished.

Patiently, he unwrapped Kathryn's preference sheet, anticipation pulsing through his veins. Months of wondering was over.

With the last flip, he scanned the sheet—a clean one where nothing had been checked off or filled in. Nothing disturbed the laser-printed letters, lines, or boxes. Nothing but a small note written thoughtfully at the bottom.

I'm not exactly sober as I write this, so bear with me. The truth is, when it comes to this world—your world—I've stared at more than one preference sheet with fierce determination, and have come to the sinking conclusion that I have no idea what I want. I didn't think I wanted to share you, or be shared by you.

Scratch that. I don't want to share you. Or be shared by you.

There. I said it.

But I also don't want you to feel the need to go somewhere else, or hide your true self. You fought your way back from death. The least I can do is love you enough to believe in us and explore. Get to know you. Know myself. Is anything less really love?

P.S. - I'm sorry I called you an ass.

P.P.S. - What do you think of fire play?

Staring at the page, Jake reread it. A few times.

What's with the sharing? And who the hell would I share with? And . . . fire play?

Obviously, Drunk Kitten had a freaky side. The one that involved multiple partners? Not happening. But the one that liked the heat?

Any day or night, kitten. Fire good.

Thinking hard, he tried to peel back the meaning behind each word. They could be the cryptic ramblings of a bender gone wrong, but

Kathryn wasn't drunk when she handed it to him. If she thought there was a chance in any universe he'd be playing *pass the kitten*, she was wrong.

He refolded the note and tucked it away. Gentle Jake wouldn't have much time—maybe a few seconds of chitchat to hash it out. Master Jake would do the convincing.

I feel a serious spanking coming up. That and a ball gag are definitely in order.

There was a certain impatience that came with being a Dom. A raw and carnal caveman side that embraced primal instincts like smacking, grabbing, nipping, sucking, licking, and last but not least, fucking. Doing all these things to unyielding satisfaction, and doing them as soon as the urge struck.

Raw, unadulterated Jake was ready to burst out. His huff more of a grunt, Jake shot to his feet and dragged his knuckles and throbbing dick up and down the halls, ready to fuck some sense into his sub.

Stay calm. It's not like she asked for a threesome.

No, it was so much worse. Somehow in her overactive imagination, the woman had convinced herself that *he* wanted a threesome.

It's bad enough that I've got three people in my head at all times as it is.

First, there was Gentle Jake. The voice of reason who insisted that with Kathryn, it was prudent to stay calm and talk things through. Then there was Master Jake, who always believed a firm hand on her beet-red ass was all the talk that was needed. Finally, as it is with all hot-blooded men, there was Caveman Jake, who tended to fall back on three simple words to solve all of life's complex problems: *must*, *fuck*, and *now*.

Every last one of the horny sides of Jake came to a screeching halt at the cafeteria. In his rush, he nearly breezed past the doorway.

But there she was. Leave it to the ponytail high on her head to give away her position. Having a casual dinner. Front and center with her fucking ex-husband, Carter.

There were a lot of things that could be explained away. Kathryn fleeing to an all-expenses penthouse getaway, courtesy of his credit card. The drunk dial at nearly four in the morning, with one-hundred-and-one ways of calling him an ass.

Even her engagement ring being tossed aside and left behind. The precious jewel that represented his renewed belief in love and marriage. Honesty and trust. A token of faith that he could actually love again. Love and be loved for who he truly was.

But *this*? Making it sound like he wanted the threesome, when all the while, it was Kathryn that wanted it. Wanted *him*. Carter fucking Reeves.

Maybe it was time to rip a page from Kathryn's playbook. His turn to walk away. Or run. For once in his life, completely bypass the big, bad Dom inside and say the word that would end this roller coaster ride once and for all.

Red.

Just walk away and let her go.

26

JAKE

On the verge of a sharp about face, Jake took a breath, flaring his nostrils as his little kitten squeezed a napkin to gingerly dab some food from Carter's smug fucking grin.

Gentle Jake and Caveman Jake took two solid steps back. Master Jake had work to do. With determined steps, the Dom in him crossed the room, ready to unleash.

"Jake!" Carter popped to his feet. "God, what a night. Kathryn was saying—"

"I don't really care what Kathryn was saying. It'll be hard for her to say much of anything with her mouth full of—"

Jake considered finishing the sentence with the words *a ball gag* or *my cock*, choked back by the quickness of his reflexes.

"Food," he finally said, taking a second to get a better look at the woman smiling up at him.

This. Isn't. Kathryn.

Laughing off his Dom aggression, Jake smiled profusely as the woman batted her bright blue eyes and swallowed a spoonful of cheesecake. Jake was still staring when Carter locked him in a hearty handshake.

Regretful, Carter continued. "Kathryn was saying she couldn't join us, and as much as I wanted to do this with her first, you're here now."

Confused, Jake repeated the statement back as a question. "Do this with her first? This what?"

"Give her the one thing she always said she needed. For me to get my head out of my ass and find happiness. Jake, this is my wife, Claire."

"Your . . . wife?" Jake hoped his poker face could stand up to the scrutiny of being eye-to-eye with this Kathryn Chase doppelganger. The resemblance was uncanny.

Strawberry-blonde. Same frame. Same height. And what were the chances this one was a nurse? By her uniform, she was.

What can I say? The man has a type.

"Congratulations. I didn't realize . . ." Jake couldn't help it. His gaze fell to the third finger on Carter's left hand. A credit to his old life, but Jake didn't miss much.

Nope. No wedding ring.

And leave it to a surgeon's attention to detail. The scrutinizing glance was noticed.

Carter rubbed his hand. "A surgeon's lot." Grinning, he tugged a gold chain out from under his shirt. A thick gold band dangled along it. "Wearing rings in surgery always poses an issue, and after a dozen hours hunched over a patient, my fingers swell like Italian sausages. Please," Carter motioned to an empty chair, "join us."

"Yes," Claire said with so much warmth, the offer was tempting.

"I wish I could," Jake said, honestly sorry to have to turn them down. "Perhaps another time. I'm trying to catch up with Kathryn."

"Last I saw her, she was in Wing E. Turned down the dinner offer to treat a patient on a gurney."

"How long ago?"

Thinking for a second, Carter shrugged. "I don't know. Ten minutes or so. How about this, you head to the lobby and I'll have her paged."

With a grateful nod, Jake took several fast steps away. "You're a lifesaver," he called out over his shoulder.

"That's what they tell me," Carter called back without a trace of modesty.

"Paging Nurse Chase. Nurse Kathryn Chase, your party is expecting you in the lobby."

Making a left at the emergency room lobby, Jake walked in, half expecting Kathryn to already be there. But if she was in the middle of a procedure, her absence was understandable.

It was the first time all day he'd really looked around. The long arrows painted along the floor provided direction to anyone who needed it, and the big blue one with the bold letter E was beckoning him.

The hall covered at least thirty rooms on each side, which Jake paced the length of twice, casual as he checked for any open doors. Each pass brought him alongside a patient sleeping on a gurney.

What did Carter say? Is this the guy Kathryn was checking on?

Gurneys in a hall? Typical. Patients on the gurneys in the hall? Less so, but under the right circumstances, it happened.

But a lone gurney in a hall when you could hear a pin drop . . . and plenty of vacant examining rooms available? Something seemed off.

He took several silent steps over, careful not to wake what looked to be a man. Even with most of the man's face covered, as soon as Jake stood over him, the salt-and-pepper military haircut was unmistakable. *Scott.*

Jake pried open each of Scott's eyes. *Responsive, thank God. Fuck.*

"Scott!" Jake pressed two fingers to the side of the detective's neck, feeling the thud of his pulse, and he let out a relieved breath. The detective's heartbeat was strong and steady. "Scott, can you hear me?"

Scott stirred, pinching his brows hard through several attempted blinks. His eyes settled and remained closed. In a long puff of air, he whispered, "Kathryn."

Looking down at Scott, all Jake could think of was Kathryn. Kathryn had been here, had come across Scott mere minutes ago. With no response to the page, Jake had to assume the worst.

His girl was missing and in danger.

He pulled out his phone and pressed the contact of the one person he knew who could get this place locked down now. After the third ring, the call picked up.

"Hey, Jake."

"Listen to me very carefully. Kathryn was working on a case. Detective Delaney is unconscious, and Kathryn is missing."

"What do we do?"

"Get the hospital completely locked down. Carter is in the cafeteria if you need him. Paco can tell me the last room Scott was in. I'll get that, text it to you, and head there now. Call the police. Let them know what's going on."

"I'm on it."

"Thanks, Julian."

27
KATHRYN

Twenty minutes earlier

Empty lobby. Quiet halls. Kathryn figured her night in the ER was just about done.

She checked in with the nurses at the entry point. Everything was under control. Doing one last walk-through, she checked silently as she moved from room to room, deciding it was just about time to call it a night and hunt down Jake.

Or hunt down Jake *to* make her night.

There was one last item on her mental checklist. She wanted to swing by Wing E, just to make sure Troy and Scott were okay and didn't need her to smuggle them some late-night offerings from the snack bar. Nutter Butters. Jell-O. Soda. All they had to do was ask and they would receive. Mama knew all the good stashes.

She turned a corner and froze when she saw Andi. Pretty, pixie-haired, long-legged Andi.

If Kathryn turned her down, not wanting to mix business with pleasure, or pleasure with pleasure, would Andi make a fuss? Cost her the teaching opportunity that had breathed new life into her otherwise mostly dull workday?

Ugh. We should talk.

Kathryn took a few hesitant steps forward as Andi wheeled a gurney through the hall, parking it along one side before taking brisk steps back in the direction she came.

"Kathryn," a man called from behind her.

Regretting her decision to turn back even before she did it, she sucked it up and painted on a smile. "Carter. Hi."

"I know you hate the accolades, but great job today," her ex said, reaching out to grab her shoulders and give them a congratulatory squeeze.

Having both his hands land on her shoulders was seriously making her itch with discomfort. Kathryn squirmed out from under them, but Carter's smile didn't dim.

"Not that that's anything new coming from you. Now, if you're ready to get off your feet for a hot second, there's a casual dinner with your name on it."

"Dinner?" Kathryn was distracted as she saw Andi stepping away from the gurney. Why would a pharmacy tech be at the hospital wheeling a gurney? Addressing Carter, she blurted, "I can't. I've got one more patient to check on."

"Want me to help?" Carter asked.

"No." Kathryn relaxed the strain in her voice and mustered up a smile. "I mean, no—you've worked ten times harder than I have today. You've earned your dinner. Another time."

"Another time. Soon," he said, playfully aiming a finger gun at her.

Kathryn could only nod, taking several rushed steps to the gurney. She glanced at the crisp white sheet pulled up to the resting man's eyes. Noting the sheet was tucked a little too high, she pulled it off his face to give him some air.

A tug of the sheet revealed an unconscious Scott, pale and lifeless. Alarmed, she called his name, and when there was no response, she administered several mild slaps to the cheek.

"Scott? Detective Delaney, can you hear me?" Nothing but a long breath.

Then he murmured, "Troy."

Shit. Troy. This couldn't have happened half an hour ago when everyone and their mother were in the hall?

Scanning in each direction, Kathryn was distressed to see the halls were empty. She raced in the direction Andi had gone, creeping along the hallway and opening each door with a near-silent knock.

She bounced from room to room, but her search turned up empty. No Andi. And no Troy. She might as well have been searching for a needle in quicksand. The process was taking way too long.

Kathryn reached for her phone—the one she'd lost that morning in the hotel room. *Goddammit.*

The nurses' station was empty. Momentarily, most likely, but at the worst possible time. Thankfully, there was a phone mounted to the wall just up ahead. Kathryn made a beeline for it and hit the red button for the security desk.

"Security," the man said, identifying himself.

"Ow!" Kathryn dropped the phone and grabbed her arm.

She mouthed the word *help*, but nothing came out. The weight of her body rested against the cool wall, sliding despite her will to fight. To stay standing. She could feel her body collapsing. As if from a great distance, she heard her name being paged.

"Paging Nurse Chase. Nurse Kathryn Chase, your party is expecting you in the lobby."

∽

When Kathryn came to, a damp rag was pressed hard against her mouth and nose. She struggled to breathe but otherwise let her limbs go limp and remained still.

She wasn't half as concerned about what was being done as the psychopath doing it. When oxygen is cut off, panic starts setting in. But she knew she had only one option to survive.

Submit. Or rather, succumb. Build the illusion her body had given in to the injection of drugs and the chloroform covering her face now.

Whatever she'd been injected with had already worn off—which could have been minutes or hours. Or days?

No. I haven't peed myself, so it can't be days. Lucky for me, chloroform doesn't work the way it does in the movies.

But why move her from the hall and give her chloroform unless . . . unless her attacker knew the shot wouldn't be enough.

Faking her sleep state and keeping her eyes shut, Kathryn waited until the footsteps moved away. Cracking her eyes open even a fraction was a risk, but a necessary one to take in every important detail of the situation she was in.

How many assailants? What did they want? How far were they willing to go to get it?

A former Army combat nurse with just enough survival, evasion, resistance, and escape training, a training every part of her exhausted body had hated at the time, Kathryn relied on the skills she'd prayed she'd never have to use. All the while grateful as hell they were there.

The good news? Only one assailant. *Andi.*

The bad news? Not only did Andi have a crash cart of drugs that were all lethal in the wrong doses, she now also had something that changed the dynamics entirely.

A five o'clock shadow.

Whether her captor was a man or a woman made no difference. Kathryn was a trained combat vet. A fierce fighting machine of a woman who knew how to take names and kick ass. No one had ever accused this hellraiser of being a lightweight.

Still, her position on the bed and the drugs in her system meant whatever advantage she might have was diminished. And her wrists being bound wasn't helping. Kathryn could feel the tug of jute ropes against them, binding them together and tethering her to the siderail of the hospital bed.

At least they're loose. Maybe loose enough to slip through.

Silently, she watched as Andi prepped a cart next to Troy and injected something into his IV. Kathryn made small, slight movements, stretching the bindings and twisting her wrists.

With a sigh, Andi set down the syringe and turned. "I know you're awake."

Then there's no use pretending.

Kathryn assessed the ropes tying her to the bed. The knot was a perfect match for the impressions in the crime-scene photographs of Troy's arms. A sophisticated knot Kathryn hadn't seen before.

"What kind of knot is this?" she asked, making whatever connection she could with her attacker.

Thoughtfully, Andi's expression warmed. "I call it Troy's Trap. I made it just for him. The harder you pull, the tighter it gets."

Instantly, Kathryn switched her technique from gentle tugging to slow wriggling.

"I don't want to hurt you," Andi said with big eyes.

"I don't want you to hurt me either," Kathryn said honestly.

Kathryn could kick her if she got any closer, but despite the looseness of her restraints, her wrists were still secured. Any attempts to free herself now would probably only piss Andi off. Maybe it was time to do what Jake and Paco and even Julian always encouraged her to do. It was time to talk. Sub to sub.

"Is it worth me saying you don't have to do this?"

Thoughtful, Andi gave her a small, crooked grin before taking a seat next to Troy. There was a strange gentleness in the way she began to stroke his chest. "I loved him. And in some way, I think he loved me too."

Kathryn's expression must have changed, because Andi lost her cool.

Adamant, she bristled, thumbing hard at her own chest. "You think I'm crazy?"

God, I hate when people ask me that. "No, it's just that . . . you wanted to give me a collar."

Wide-eyed, Andi bristled. "*Give* you a collar? No. *Sell* you a collar. Yes. Just trying to make a living." Blinking in disbelief, Andi balked. "Why would a sub collar another sub?"

Kathryn hoped the question was rhetorical, because at this point, she had no idea and wished that BDSM came with a manual.

Shrugging, Kathryn changed the subject, stating, "I don't think you're crazy," because she had a deep-rooted sense that crazy people needed that validation. She could only hope her kidnapper was buying it.

"He loves me," Andi said again, emphasizing each word. "Why do you think he's been making up descriptions of how I look? How could I possibly look that different each and every time?"

Kathryn's thoughts spun. Andi was right. Troy had described the women so differently. Each and every time. And he'd also said she was petite, which Andi definitely was not.

Paco had said it best. *For all he knew, they were completely different women*. But Troy did know. He knew his assailant wasn't a woman.

"His precious goddamned public image. Troy was too afraid of how the public would react if they knew he swung both ways, especially with a trans woman." Andi sneered. "The girlfriend? She knew too."

"She knew about you?" Shocked, Kathryn pressed her lips together hard to shut up.

"Knew about me?" Andi scoffed. "Alexis arranged for me." Gently, she slid her fingers through Troy's hair. "Brought me in. Had a fucking black book of all the deep, dark, dirty little things this boy likes to do. Trust me, I took care of him. Too well."

"Alcohol injections?"

Andi shrugged. "Sometimes it worked, but I kept overshooting the vein. Burns like shit and gives a fraction of the buzz. But he wanted to keep it going."

"You risked a lot. Doing it at Club Lazarus." It was a gamble. But Kathryn needed her speculation validated, and addressing it head-on was the only way to know for sure. "Why there?"

"Troy's idea. Hidden but still fed his need to be seen, among other things. The best of both worlds. And if anyone suspected he was drinking—like his manager, who knew more about Troy than his own mother—they didn't have to worry about him drinking there. Everyone knows there's no alcohol at the club. I would've done anything for him."

"Troy was going to leave his fiancée for you?"

A pitying look flashed across Andi's face as she crossed her legs, the *What universe to you live in?* written in the crease that formed in her brow.

"No," she said flatly. "He wanted to keep our arrangement going. I was okay with it too, until Alexis realized we'd developed feelings for each other. Hell hath no fury . . ."

Kathryn paused for a second from working the ropes, a relief to the raw skin around her wrists. "She threatened you?"

"That's not nearly imaginative enough for the likes of Alexis Kennedy. She's got money, but he has so much more. She made sure everything he and I did together was videoed."

"Blackmail?" Kathryn kept talking. Her wrist was nearly free.

"Alexis wanted everything. The ten-carat wedding ring. Mansion. House full of kids. It was an image that suddenly didn't include me, so I threatened to expose everything. That's when he turned against me," Andi said, her face anguished and twisting.

"He came to my place. Walked in my house. Took me to my bed, and beat me. Almost killed me. Months with my jaw wired shut gave me time to think. Well . . ." Andi swiped away a tear, clasping her hands, and looped them around one knee. "You want me to be the bad guy? I'll be the bad guy. For months, I woke up in cold sweats and with tremors. He haunted my dreams. Now, it's time this villain haunts every last motherfucking one of his."

Andi looked toward the gurney and picked up a scalpel. "I'm sorry, Mr. Brooks. I'm afraid children aren't going to be possible for you."

When Andi stood up and turned to face Troy, Kathryn took her shot, springing up and kicking as hard and high as she could, catching Andi in the jaw. The force threw Andi across the room, along with the scalpel.

Unfortunately, all Kathryn had accomplished was to enrage the nut job now set on causing Kathryn harm.

Andi lunged. Ready with another kick, Kathryn thrust her foot at Andi, landing her leg squarely in her strong, waiting hands.

"Gotcha," Andi said, now licking blood from her lip. And she did.

Kathryn couldn't move without losing her balance, and even an inch in the wrong direction reminded her that Andi had her.

A sadistic smile stretched across Andi's face. "Feisty for a sub. Don't worry, Nurse Chase. I've got the cure. And it won't be that baby dose I gave you earlier. A syringe full of propofol should do the trick."

With Kathryn's leg secured in one arm, Andi managed to flip her around, landing her stomach on the bed. Andi's heavy body crashed over her, keeping Kathryn still as Andi fished through the drug cart.

"Stay still," she snapped. She gave Kathryn's ass an angry, hard smack, and Kathryn froze. "That's for kicking my jaw."

"I'm sorry," Kathryn huffed out, knowing her sincere apology wouldn't mean much, but she gave it anyway. Seeing the syringe, she sucked in a breath. "That much will kill me."

Andi leaned closer to speak into Kathryn's ear. "Someone taught me that a little needle can cause a lot of pain. And I'm a girl of my word. I don't want to hurt you. If you move even the slightest bit, I'll make it hurt. If you don't, I'll keep the pain to a minimum. I don't want to pump all of it in you, but if you so much as breathe funny, I will. Now, take your medicine and stay still."

28

KATHRYN

With her eyes shut tightly, Kathryn held her breath and choked back a sob.

What if I never see Jake again? What if this is it?

Too many thoughts and memories flickered through her mind. Jake's body. One second lifeless and shredded with bullets, and the next, alive. So alive. His hands on her skin when she didn't know who he was. His lips on her mouth. Those dark, penetrating hazel eyes. His warm, musky scent that was part of him—in his car, on his clothes, in his office chair. That spicy mix that always let Kathryn know she was loved and cherished. That she was safe.

"Jake," she whispered through tight lips behind the darkness of her closed eyes. A tear ran down her cheek as his scent surrounded her. But it wasn't a vibrant memory in her mind. It was *actually* him.

"Breathe," he said low, his words commanding her.

She sucked in a breath and opened her eyes. He held a police-issued Glock aimed right at Andi's head.

"Andi," Jake said loudly, his voice angry but controlled. "Because you need the practice, stick the syringe in the pillow, empty it, then get the fuck off her and back away."

Kathryn bit her lip as Andi complied. As soon as a hundred sixty pounds of lean muscle moved off her, Kathryn rushed behind Jake.

"Here," he said, pulling her phone from his back pocket. "Julian's taken point."

She pressed favorite number two. *Spouse.*

After half a ring, he picked up the call. "Kathryn?" In just her name, she could hear Julian's worry and fear.

"Yes, Julian. I'm fine," she said through trembling lips.

Jake slid an arm around Kathryn's waist, keeping her close against him. She filled her lungs with air, then let it all out with a shuddering breath as her head dropped onto the strength of his chest.

"Where are you?"

"Send security to . . ." She scanned the whiteboard on the wall and said, "Room 432," then disconnected the call, staring hard for a second at the length of rope still bound to the siderail on the gurney. The one she'd slipped from to free herself.

"Kathryn?" Jake asked. "What is it?"

Her brow shot high. Wide-eyed, she mouthed the words, "The ropes."

Jake's whisper was a rush of heat against her ear. "I've got plenty."

The knot she'd unraveled was one she'd seen at the club. There was a reason Paco wanted to get to the bottom of the case first.

This was the reason.

Not a cover-up. Protection. The same protectiveness that ran as strong through Jake's veins as it did hers.

With a pen from the table, Kathryn jabbed at the heart of the tight knot, loosened it, then dropped the short length of jute down her blouse, removing a huge bread crumb that would point straight to Club Lazarus.

Jake frowned, that worried crease she knew so well forming between his brows. "You sure?"

His question was valid. Hiding evidence was just the start of a string of lies to the authorities. But that wasn't what he meant.

"It might be in vain," he said as he glanced at Andi.

He was right. One word from Andi, and it was game over.

Kathryn met Andi's dark stare with a penetrating gaze. Could the woman who nearly killed her be reasonable? "Andi—"

"Let me guess. In another minute, if those ropes are still there, they'll lead the police investigation back to the club, which would give the cops the justification to seize their records. Records that could become public." Andi's gaze turned cold. "You'd go this far to protect Troy?"

"Not him," Kathryn said, taking a step forward before Jake pulled her back, his gun still trained on the dangerous assailant. "Everyone. Everyone who believes the club is their safe place. Their sanctuary."

"Where our secrets are protected," Jake said, his voice persuasive and convincing.

"Fine." Andi raised her hands in surrender. "I'll leave the ropes and the club out of it."

"You will?" Kathryn asked, surprised.

"Don't be so shocked, Nurse Chase. It's one less piece of evidence against me. And like I said, I never wanted to hurt you. Or anyone. Just the one person who hurt me."

Two armed guards stormed into the room. Jake discreetly lowered the pistol out of sight, a weapon that belonged to Detective Scott Delaney. A cop's gun in a civilian's hand wouldn't go over well with the police. His move was solely to protect Scott.

Jake ushered Kathryn from the room as they secured Andi. "We'll need to stick around. Give our statements." His words were an apology, taking the full weight of everything that had happened to her—and was happening still—on his very broad, unbelievably strong shoulders.

She curled into the reassuring warmth of his hold, finally able to let go of a trembling breath. "Is it your mission to protect everyone?"

Jake's hand slipped along her jaw, cradling her cheek. "Not everyone," he said, looking at her so intently, she knew it would be a while before he let her drift more than an inch from him.

Her heart began to pound, a frantic, eager, *want you to take me for the rest of my life* rhythm she hoped he could hear with his heart.

By his crushing, desperately rough kiss that explored every corner of her mouth, he could.

29

KATHRYN

Blindfolded, Kathryn couldn't help asking the question for the millionth time. "Can't you at least give me a hint?"

Call her antsy, but yesterday's brush with death had made her that much more eager to soak in time with Jake. True, blindfolded counted. But not when he was driving, and she was a car seat away. It might as well be a million miles away. And punishing her with a firm no-touching rule while in transit was barbaric.

"Not a chance, kitten. But don't worry, we're almost there."

Instead of taking his truck, Jake had insisted on the Bugatti, a sleek sports car with a dangerous blend of power and style that so perfectly mirrored her man.

And the sinfully red off-the-shoulder gown she wore felt like a cloud next to her skin. She loved it more than when she first saw it in *Vogue*, immediately ripping out the page and sticking it in a drawer. Her *someday if I need a gown for a ball* drawer that she was sure Jake never took an interest in.

The smooth vibration in her seat rumbled a little stronger before dying away as Jake killed the engine. "Okay, the blindfold stays on. That's an order," he said, his voice stern but warm.

"Yes, Master Jake," she said, letting the rasp of her voice linger suggestively.

The heat of his lips met hers as he pressed a kiss to them before he climbed out of the car. As soon as her door opened, he unfastened her seatbelt and lifted her into the familiar cradle of his arms.

Her man being sexy? Perhaps. *Or he just knows the klutz in me is prone to fall flat on my ass in heels.*

Kathryn dangled her feet with glee as she wrapped her arms around his neck. "When will the blindfold come off?"

"If you keep asking, tomorrow," he said with a chuckle.

"Oh, good. The blindfold comes off when I get to wear underwear again. It must be Christmas."

She didn't realize they weren't alone until she heard the deep rumble of, "Hey, Jake. Your girl looks beautiful."

"Julian?" she asked.

"Hi, Kathryn. Or should I say Lolita?"

That made her giggle.

"In three months, you'll all be saying Mrs. Russo," Jake said proudly before setting her on her feet. Untying her blindfold, he whispered in her ear. "This is ours, kitten."

Kathryn took a moment, recognizing and yet not recognizing the impressive building they stood in front of. Then she realized it was the building she'd seen in the architectural drawings. The ones she wasn't supposed to have seen.

Breathless, she asked, "Ours?"

It was her own version of the stunning museum in Austria. The Kunsthaus Bregenz, with block walls of solid stone for the first two floors, and glorious semi-frosted and clear dark windows leading up to the sky.

Kathryn took careful steps into the building, smiling at several people standing in the elegant lobby, the men decked out in suits, and a woman in a gorgeous blush-colored gown with her dark wavy hair swept up. And then there was Julian, looking way too elegant wearing Kathryn's favorite blouse.

Her smile spread wide as they all seemed to be standing before her and Jake, not moving to greet her, embrace her, or even shake her hand.

"What's going on?" she asked.

Smiling, Paco stepped out from behind the small crowd. "It would appear that Jake Russo and Kathryn Chase have become partners in a new venture of luxury national and international BDSM clubs, with several co-owners, of course."

"You?" she asked Paco as Jake wrapped an arm around her waist.

"Not just me. Everyone in this room."

Jake explained. "I figured we needed a place for us. But as soon as I started talking about it, everyone wanted in. Kathryn, meet Corey and Crystal. Corey has his own investigative firm. He's the guy I call when I need to know anything and everything about people."

"Everything?" Kathryn asked as a warmth stole up her cheeks.

"Don't worry. Your secrets are safe with me," Corey said with a wink. "And this is my wife, Crystal."

"What the hell is it you do, Crystal?" Jake asked. "Funny, we each had a bio, and yours was mysteriously blank."

A giddy laugh came from both Paco and Crystal, but all she would say is, "Oh, not much. I find ways to keep busy. My main job is to keep this guy in his place." The stunning woman smiled through dark ruby lips before planting a lip print on Corey's cheek.

Kathryn tried not to stare, but the collar around Corey's neck said it all. Crystal was his Mistress, and the foreboding man with a myriad of tattoos and impressive muscles was her sub. A strange connection Kathryn sensed in an instant.

Corey broke from the intensity of his wife's stare. "And with our underground contacts, we've amassed a waiting list of over a thousand clients worldwide, ready to plunk down their cold, hard cash for the price of admission. I've already vetted most of them."

"What is the price of admission?" Kathryn asked.

"More than the price of the car you and Jake rolled up in," Julian said.

Her mouth dropped open. "Per member?"

"Per year." Julian waggled his brows, oddly comfortable with an arrangement that would keep his squat-tightened butt out. "It's luxury BDSM, and it's the future."

"Luxury BDSM," she asked. "Is there such a thing?"

"There is now." Julian brightened, warming to the topic. "The most exclusive, secretive, elite clubs focused on providing a total experience. Exotic getaways that you can only reach by private jets, yachts, or helicopters. With exquisite five-star cuisine and full spa packages including custom massages and on-site beauty care."

"Wow. And people will pay this price?"

"Yes. People with fetishes and obscene amounts of money. Plus, how else can I keep the growing list of exes out?"

"You?"

Julian preened. "Girl, you are looking at the spokesperson."

Kathryn let the idea sink in, nodding in agreement. "My best friend, the face of luxury BDSM. Did you wish really hard? Or sell your soul to the devil?"

"Not only did he, but I accepted." Paco donned a salacious grin. "Julian is trustworthy. Loyal. Went through the agony of Corey's background check, a polygraph, and a forensic investigation of his finances. And he agreed to all of it without knowing what any of it was for. Only that Jake had requested it. Plus, his knowledge of clubs and the lifestyle is impressive. And coming from me, that's saying a lot."

"It means he'll be getting his own black card and will finally give me mine back." Jake held out a waiting hand.

"After mine comes in," Julian said hopefully.

Jake rolled his eyes before he continued. "And it was Paco's idea to go big or go home, so if we're doing it, how about something international? A brand. From the Rocky Mountains to Fifth Avenue. Paris to Milan. Europe. Asia. South America. There are even a few spots in Africa that might warrant a look-see. Even Fiji."

Kathryn's excited squeal was deafening. "It's amazing. But what will we call it?"

"Don't worry. Corey and Crystal have a few names they're toying with," Jake said. "But before we do anything more, we need to christen it."

Kathryn giggled, lowering her voice as she asked, "With sex?"

"Among other things," Jake said, agreeing in no uncertain terms. "But first, with this."

Paco stepped forward, opening a long box so Kathryn could see what was inside. The piece of jewelry sparkling on the dark velvet inside should require a retina warning—a dozen strands of diamonds looped through an eternity shape along the front.

Breathless, Kathryn slid her fingers along the fine piece of jewelry. "It's stunning."

"Consider yourself owned," Jake said, removing it from the box. "For our first collaring ceremony in the new space, if you'll have it. And me . . . as your Dom." He lifted her chin. "And yours alone.

Teary, Kathryn nodded. "Yes."

She lifted the length of her hair aside as Jake cinched the collar gently to her neck. He followed with a tender peck before spinning her around, cupping her jaw, and pressing a kiss to her lips.

A round of applause filled the room, and Julian handed them each a flute of champagne as he made the rounds. "Drink up before this place institutes its no-alcohol policy."

"Now," Jake said, "Julian will give us all a tour so you can decide what room you'd like to christen first. And one of them might be a little hotter than the rest."

"Fire play?" she asked.

Jake nodded. "Your preference sheet is my command."

Less shy than ever, and eager to tie up a very loose end, Kathryn rubbed her nose to his. "None."

"None?" he asked in disbelief.

"Nope. I love you, Jake. And I love this," she said, smoothing a finger along the diamond collar around her neck. "But I don't want our first time to be in any of these rooms."

Surprised, he lifted a brow. "You don't?"

Kathryn shook her head, letting a devilish smile break free. "I'd like to get out of here. Break this property in right. I'll bet from just the right outside wall, we can watch the sun set over Pike's Peak."

With a deep breath, Jake took her glass and set both of them aside before he unbuttoned his blazer and whisked her back in his arms.

"Until the blindfold comes out again." With a few determined steps to Kathryn's first real scene, Jake growled. "For the next hour, only three things can move past your lips, little sub," he said sternly as he smiled.

"*Mm-hmm.*" She nodded attentively.

"Your safe word. Yes, sir. And my cock."

The evening breeze was electric along her body as he walked them outside, moving to the west side of the building before he set her feet on the grass.

Into her ear, he murmured, "Do you understand?"

Kathryn's eyes fell closed as her fingers skated around the collar. The one that made her his, with the promise of eternity. With the love of her life. Her Dom.

There was nothing more to say except, "Yes, sir."

∾

Thank you for reading *RISING*! I hope you loved the ongoing story of Jake and Kathryn.

Ready for a taste of something a little Ruthless?

Power plays are hard.

Trying to one up the stranger who banged me senseless last night? *Definitely harder.*

Available on All Platforms! **Get RUTHLESS WARS Now>**

"*Tons of chemistry and passion ... Highly addictive*" ~*Goodreads Reviewer*

∾

Looking for another sexy billionaire?

Meet Davis R. Black … aka Richard. Some know him as a tech

mogul. To Jaclyn, he's the King of the A-holes. Which is why this billionaire is hiding *his* in plain sight. Check out the first book in the Ruthless Billionaires Club.

Available on All Platforms! **Get RUTHLESS GAMES now!**
Flip the page to check out a preview.

∾

Need another fix of steamy suspense? The hot and steamy ALEX DRAKE SERIES with Alex, Madison, and Paco Robles is available on Amazon! **Get ACCESS Now>>>**

When seclusive billionaire Alex Drake sets his sights on Madison, obsession takes over. Unlocking his world was easy. Seducing her was inevitable. But securing her heart might be impossible. He's ready to give in to her every desire except for one. The only thing she wants. An answer. To a tiny question. Why her?

Get ACCESS Now>>>

∾

Join Lexxi's VIP reader list to be the first to know of new releases, special prices, and get freebies every week on all platforms!

Free hot romances & happily ever afters delivered to your inbox.
https://www.lexxijames.com/freebies

RUTHLESS GAMES

CHAPTER 1

"Have you ever been obsessed?" he asked.

With the midday sun blazing into his new uptown Dallas office, Richard noticed Margot squinting. He grabbed a remote control. At the press of a button, transparent screens dropped over two walls of windows, softly dimming the sunlight while capturing the panoramic skyscraper views. When her eyes adjusted, she resumed her skeptical scowl.

He couldn't help firing such a pointed question at her. And not just for shock effect. He was revealing a secret truth that no matter how hard he tried, he couldn't escape.

Appearing unimpressed, she stared back. "Players like you don't get obsessed. You get fleeting infatuations, until the next new set of bouncy breasts catch your eye."

He took the jab in stride. Impressing Margot wasn't the goal. Convincing her to join him was. She had a knack for cutting to the chase, a quality he respected.

Facts. Numbers.
All business. No bullshit.
Here we go.

Despite the expansiveness of his fortieth-floor office, they sat a cozy distance from each other, each on a matching tufted black leather sofa, with a low glass table between them. Two chilled Voss waters waited an arm's length away on granite coasters.

The refreshments weren't just there because of the sweltering Texas heat outside. Richard knew the drill. Margot demanded complete sobriety during any negotiation, and this wasn't exactly a social call. With her golden hair perfectly layered in an expensive cut, and a custom suit contouring her svelte body and complementing her delicate features, she was a woman of the world. No doubt about it—her razor-sharp mind analyzed him. Each word. Every move.

And he knew exactly why.

Jumping on this crazy train would take a wish and a prayer, and a butt-load of cash. And crazy wasn't even the half of it.

Illegal? *Definitely not.*

Well, maybe.

Okay, probably.

Richard tried to stay out of anything that was blatantly against the law, but everything about this plan screamed lawsuit. Big, fat, fucking lawsuit. And if the media caught wind of it? He'd definitely be kissing his own ass good-bye. His ass *and* his assets.

He promptly shoved all the risks from his mind, focusing on the ultimate prize. "It's not fleeting. And Jaclyn Long isn't remotely close to a flash in the pan. Any day now, she could take over Long Multinational Systems, and we both know if that happens, it's game over. This is my chance. My *only* shot."

When Margot's gaze remained unimpressed, he decided to change tactics. *Bring out the big guns. Honesty.*

"I'm used to women looking at me a certain way," he said. "Like a gift-wrapped lottery ticket they want to unwrap with their teeth. Half the time they see me as a sugar daddy, and the other half as a baby daddy. But when Jaclyn looked at me, it was different. Like I wasn't worth her time. But she's definitely worth mine."

Margot's brow lifted.

"Here." He opened the folder on the coffee table between them and handed her a few documents. "I'm ready to hit her with all I've got, but she can't see me coming."

Margot skimmed the pages, her smile spreading wider as she flipped page after page.

"You've known me a long time, Margot. If I'm in it, I'm in it to win it. But I need an advantage. You're one of the few people who live in her inner circle."

"Lived," she said, correcting him as she returned the documents and resumed her stoic expression. "It's been a while."

Her practiced poker face made it impossible to get the slightest hint of where she stood. But she was listening, and his instincts kicked in, prompting him to hit the "schmooze" button.

"But you know Jaclyn better than anyone," he said. "Maybe better than she knows herself. To make this work, I need you on my side."

Margot looked up for a second, contemplating a response. Sinking back into the fine leather, she crossed her legs and stretched an arm along the low back of the couch. "And exactly what's that shot worth to you, Richard?"

Well, that was fast. He figured she'd at least hear him out on the details of this scheme. But, nope. She was ready to decide if she was in or out, and it all came down to price. Her casual indifference telegraphed that she knew his position as well as he did. Without a lick of leverage, why pretend?

Richard leaned forward, resting his elbows on his knees. "How about we cut to the chase? Name your price."

She smiled, its immediacy killing any hope he had for a fair and reasonable negotiation. "*Whether* you pull this off or not, I get five percent of your company."

His eyes popped. Margot's hardball game wasn't just in a league all its own. It was like she'd invented the fucker.

He opened his mouth to counter, but the subtle lift of her elegant hand stopped him cold.

"That's nonnegotiable," she said. "And I'll need to see it in writing today. I'll also need five million in good faith money deposited to one of my accounts. Nonrefundable. My attorneys will draw up the paperwork to ensure there's no way I'm implicated if anything goes awry with this 'foolproof' plan of yours. Because what could possibly go wrong, right?"

Her sarcasm was cutting. She reached for a bottle, delicately unscrewed the cap, and sipped, letting him mull it over.

He pulled in a breath. "How about—"

"Nonnegotiable, Richard. I'm not the one who's obsessed."

Their eyes met, and hers sparkled with the triumph of a woman who knew she had him by the balls.

Margot didn't wait for his reply. "Good. Then there's the issue of your appearance."

"Hang on. A ten-thousand-dollar suit isn't good enough for Your Highness?"

She shook her head. "Oh, it's great for me, but I'm not the one you have to worry about." She swept a hand to indicate his appearance. "*Her* Highness will see you coming from a mile away. No wonder she avoided you like e. coli. Guys like you swarm her in droves. Hot. Charming. Sexy, with a naughty side that keeps girls coming back for more."

Richard gave her a not-so-modest grin.

"Absolutely worthless," Margot said sharply, quashing his smile. "Like you rolled off the latest playboy cookie-cutter assembly line. Guys like you have burned her a few times too many. So, if you want this to work, then you're going to need to make a few changes."

Damn her. Margot was enjoying this a bit too much.

He crossed his arms casually over his chest, barely wrinkling the custom-made suit. "Fine. We can work on wardrobe. What else?"

She set down her water and moved to take a seat by his side. "Hmm." She scanned his face. "I'm not partial to facial hair for this little caper."

His hand protectively flew to his scruff, and he rubbed it thoughtfully. The trademark of his signature look, gone?

"Okay. Fine. It'll grow back," he said. "Any more changes?"

She tilted her head, studying him. "I definitely see you as a blond."

Tall, dark, and handsome Richard stripped down to a squeaky-clean choirboy? He hated everything about it.

But he had to admit, the idea was bizarrely genius, and exactly what he'd asked for. Jaclyn Long would never see him coming. Literally.

Richard sighed. "All right. Fine. I'll get my stylist on it."

"Try to get it as close to my color as possible. So people might mistake us for siblings." Margot ran her fingers through his thick hair, uncharacteristically playful as she deliberately tousled his perfectly gelled waves.

Scowling, he pulled away and stood, quickly smoothing back his hair as he crossed the room. He picked up two boxes from his desk and returned, handing her one.

Margot's eyes widened the slightest bit. "I do love gifts." She popped open the box and pulled out a card.

"Scan that. It will load an encrypted app to your phone that works like FaceTime. Then, it's just a quick click to communicate with me through these." He opened the other box and pulled out a pair of titanium-framed glasses, then slid them on.

"Oh, I like those. They make you look even less like yourself."

He frowned. "Nice. And I love how looking less like myself somehow became the goal. After spending the better part of a decade honing my image, I thought I'd be seizing the day in style. But, for what's on the line, consider it done."

"And one last thing, Richard." Margot's usually stoic demeanor turned cheery. "No lies."

Confused, he cocked his head, wondering how she'd missed the gist of the entire conversation. "Uh, that might be an issue, Margot."

Her lips twitched with the smallest of smirks. "You can only take this game so far, and every sport has rules. Your name will be a mystery, and your makeover will be epic, but absolutely no lies. Nothing that can ever be used against you later—in a court of law or otherwise. Lies are too hard to keep up with, and nine times out of ten, they'll bite you in that Adonis backside of yours. You'll look and act the part of an altar boy, but that devil in you will swear to tell the truth. Maybe not the whole truth, but nothing but the truth."

She lifted her bottle for a toast. "Deal?"

He grabbed his water bottle, removed the cap, and clinked it against hers. "Deal. To the future."

"The future."

CHAPTER 2

Three guys walked into a bar . . . It had all the makings of a lame joke.

From her perch on her stool, Jaclyn used the art deco mirror hidden behind the mountain range of booze to inconspicuously spy. People-watching, she loved. Having them watch her back, not so much.

A recovering insomniac, she'd made her way down to the basement tavern at the Joule Hotel desperately needing to unwind enough to get a few hours of sleep. A nightcap wrapped in the soothing ambience of peace and quiet gave her room to breathe. Sneaking in at 1:00 a.m., not long before closing time, usually gave her all the privacy in the world, but not tonight. The inebriated band of makeshift brothers who'd just walked in promised to interrupt her laid-back plans.

She studied the trio as they found a nearby table to ogle her from. By their middle-school glances and huddled and hushed chatting, something was brewing, and it smelled all too familiar. She'd suddenly become the grand prize at the end of a pickup line.

Her thick, wavy jet-black hair that trailed clear to her ass always had a knack for catching wandering gazes. Never accused of being rail thin, Jaclyn had ample assets and voluptuous curves with a magnetic pull all their own. Add to that her bulging bank account and seductive spontaneity, only three types of men ever seemed to plow into her life.

First, there were the money-hungry, status-chasing Ivy Leaguers who pursued her like an Olympic gold medal—as if their years of hard work pinnacled in such a worthy award. These trophy hunters loved the chase, not only to capture and keep such an exotic specimen of woman, but to cage her as well. Like with all confident, capable women, captivity clashed with her charisma.

Taking second place were the uninteresting, unintelligible, garden-variety Neanderthals who traveled in packs and swarmed her in droves. They were less interested in her money and more drawn to her milkshake. Brainlessly so. Despite her best efforts to bind those babies down, her double Ds always brought the wrong sorts of boys to the yard. And this band of bar boozers plopped squarely into this bucket.

But option number three was her weakness. The consummate looks-so-good, feels-even-better bad boy. The edgy kind of guy who wasn't the right fit, but it never deterred her from forcing that puzzle piece in. Deep, deep in.

Ideal for the occasional tawdry and tantalizing tryst, they were perfect in the heat of the moment. It was those disappointing minutes afterward that always burst her bubble. For these good-time guys, both their heads had the attention span of an egg timer.

Even if she could grab their focus, she could never keep it. Sure, the sex was smoking hot. But after spending ten or twenty minutes satisfying his, um, ego, what more was there to do? Even if the owner of the down-and-dirty hot body could carry on a conversation, they rarely did. She'd succumb to the eventual boredom, and they'd be on to their next Betty. The blazing-hot boy-toy trail had become one buzzkill after another.

She watched in the mirror as the men across the room metaphorically drew straws for who would belly up to the bar beside her first.

Feeling frisky, she set her sights on a good time. Her way. And not in an annoying, pissed-off sort of spirit where her bitch face preceded her words. She had way more creativity than to waste her energy on irritation. After a long couple of days at work, a round of lighthearted entertainment seemed just the ticket to blow off a little steam.

These guys were overpreparing to the nth degree, and her mind and mood were ready to roll out the welcome mat. Between their clustered discussion and round of locker-room fist bumps, these chumps promised a few rounds of priceless stress relief.

The first of the three, who'd be the alpha if he could spell it, strolled over with his slicked-back hair, chiseled good looks, and smug grin. "Hi, sexy. Can I buy you a drink?"

God, if there was one thing Jaclyn loved, it was when d-bags didn't disappoint. She smiled adoringly, fully sizing up every arrogant inch of him.

"Well, I was just drinking water." She walked her fingers across the lacquered wood before smoothing her hand over the back of his. Her thick, come-hither lashes batted as she peered through them. "Can I ask you a question?"

He tucked his index finger under her chin, using the opportunity to flex his bicep in a shirt that was clearly two sizes too small. "Anything, sexy."

She was sure the octave of his voice just lowered. *I guess his balls just dropped.*

With a coy smile, she wrapped her hands around his taut arm. "You're *so* strong. I'll bet you play sports, right?"

He nodded, daring to brush her hair off her shoulder, caressing her arm with his rather rough hand.

Dammit, this gorilla is snagging my blouse. She wriggled out of his grasp but leaned forward, knowing the length of his stay, like his manhood, wouldn't be long.

"Well, I was thinking you'd be the perfect man. I mean, for my kids. I have five."

His face fell as he leaned back. But he wasn't getting away just yet.

She grabbed one of his grubby paws, yanking it to palm her stomach. "And one on the way!"

It was like watching a tug-of-war as he tried to get his hand back from her two-fisted grip.

"Hey, what are you doing now?" she asked innocently. "Would you like to meet them? And maybe stay till breakfast? My babysitter is about to bail, and you look like you'd be great with them. Especially the twins. Their sleep pattern is all kinds of off, and I really need some z's."

It was just the reverse pickup line to shrivel his tail. He bailed without a word.

What, no good-bye? She turned back toward the bar and watched through the mirror as he encouraged contender number two, who was now looking her way.

Contestant number two, come on down!

Strolling up, what this guy lacked in a buff bod he more than made up for in a suffocating cloud of Axe body spray.

Curse that company for making an aerosol.

He plopped on the seat next to her. "Excuse me. I couldn't help but notice you from across the room. I mean, that outfit really looks hot on you." He leaned in. "How about I buy you a drink? What can I get you?"

What do you know? He's a closer.

Well, two could play at that game.

Jaclyn settled on a more direct approach. Despite his best attempt at bravado, his bouncing leg and inability to hold eye contact revealed his nervousness. She swiveled her bar stool toward him, crossing her legs and giving him a front-row view. Her shapely calves and lower thighs poured from beneath the hem of her skirt.

"Well, maybe." Leaning in and letting her breasts test the buttons of her blouse, she pitched her voice in a breathy and demanding tone. "The last guy I dated could hold an erection for two and a half hours, cock ring and Cialis free. God, what I wouldn't give for a long, steady pony ride."

She put her hand on his tapping leg, stopping the bouncing dead in its tracks. "I'm game if you are, stud, but you will be judged. And bound."

He stumbled off his stool and scurried back to the pack.

What about my drink? Oh well.

Next!

As bachelor number three casually strolled her way, he did something unexpected. He connected with her in the mirror, his bright blue gaze locked and loaded on hers.

Men were usually too busy gawking at her assets to make real eye contact. She wasn't quite sure what to do with him, a rare breed of classic guy-next-door that she thought didn't exist outside of sitcom reruns and Hallmark movies.

There was something about him. Magnetic despite his demeanor. She just couldn't put her finger on it.

The way he looked at her. Carried himself. Brimming with casual comfort. Like she could drop by and ask him to mow her lawn, and he'd do it. And whether "mow her lawn" was code for taking her in a hot hour of ecstasy or actually trimming the grass outside her house, she could oddly see him diving into either scenario.

Please don't reek of cheap cologne.

At the bar, he barely tapped the seat next to her, asking politely, "May I?"

Jaclyn took the opportunity to get a better look. The glasses were a poor disguise for an obviously gorgeous man. He reminded her of a blond Clark Kent. How the hell Lois Lane never saw the sizzling hottie behind the thick-framed spectacles was beyond her. She also noticed his suit was nice, but hardly a Tom Ford fit or expense. It hung on the body of a well-built but not overly made-up man.

"Why not? Everyone else has."

Playing this one a little cooler wasn't exactly planned. More like a desperate measure to cover for how hot she was getting. *Like gazing into the sun.* She tore open a straw to sip her water, hoping to quell the blush rising up her face.

He sat on the stool and leaned closer, keeping his back to the two men watching. "Listen, I'm sorry about this, but those guys and I sort of made a bet on who could buy you a drink."

"Oh. I was wondering about all the action I was getting tonight. I figured the billboard I took out in the men's room was finally paying off." She trained her eyes forward, pretending interest in the bar's bourbon selection.

"I'll go. Again, I'm really sorry."

He swiveled to leave, but stopped as she softly said, "Hang on." Perusing the shelf of enticing glass bottles, she asked, "What's the wager?"

He loosened his collar a bit before answering and slowly blew out a breath. "Five hundred dollars."

"Each?" Jaclyn's lip curled up in amusement. "So, I assume if you buy me a drink, I get half, right?"

A glimmer of hope rose in his tone. "Um, yes. Of course."

She tapped her fingernails against the cool wall of the water glass, drawing a fingertip through a few drops of condensation. "I have an idea. Why not go back to them, say you thought about it, and I seemed ready to accept, but you got cold feet. Nervous."

"Nervous? To buy a woman a drink?"

"I don't know. Worried I might expect more. And you're misleading me. Wing it." She bit her bottom lip. "See if they'll take the bait."

"Bait for what?" he asked softly, questioning her reflection.

She spoke to the mirror, keeping her voice low. "The bait to up the ante." She slipped the straw to her lips, sucking another sip through her confident smile.

He leaned in, shoulder to shoulder, speaking in dramatically hushed tones. "So, you want me to hustle them?"

"Mm-hmm." Her coy look caught his.

"Before I dive headfirst into the short con of a mastermind, can I at least know your name?"

Can you at least tear off your tie? "Jaclyn."

"Richard," he said, then headed back to the huddled men who'd just become his marks.

Jaclyn watched, impressed as he really seemed to be milking it. She was nearly giddy, inwardly cheering him on as his animated chatter continued. Between their insistent nods and his "oh no, I couldn't possibly" posture, her anticipation flipped to elation at the sight of them shoving cash into his hands.

She faintly heard, "Yeah, if you get this, you've earned it."

He quickly tucked the cash in his wallet and walked back to Jaclyn in a decidedly cocky, almost pimp-walk manner.

"Well, Mr. DiCaprio, what are you up to?" she asked as he reclaimed his seat.

He again leaned in, a bit closer than the last time. The man smelled wonderful. A blend of subtle cologne, a freshness that must be his laundry, and an undertone of something that could only be described as him.

"Feel free to call me Leo, and we're up to two grand. I'm really hoping I can buy you a drink now, because I'm on a double-or-nothing deal with these guys. I'd really hate to be out four grand for the short pleasure of your company."

The blue of his softly pleading eyes sent her thoughts straight south, making her wonder if he tasted as good as he smelled. She looked over to see the bartender watching, wide-eyed and curious for her answer.

"I guess you can buy a girl a drink."

The bartender breathed a loud sigh of relief, causing both her and Richard to laugh.

"I'll take my usual, Jim."

The bartender nodded. "And for you, sir?"

"I'll have what she's having."

The bartender handed them two tumblers of Kentucky's best bourbon, and they clinked a toast.

Jaclyn sipped hers, thoroughly enjoying the aroma before letting a "mmm" escape on the exhale. Her coconspirator, on the other hand, took a sip, then desperately tried to muffle the choking that jerked to a cough.

"You okay?" she asked as she patted his back. Her patting turned to petting before she yanked her hand back. *Damn, he's built.*

"Yeah, fine," he said in a gruff voice, clearing his throat.

The bartender handed him a water, and he took a grateful sip.

"So, you're Richard. Richard what?" she asked.

The question seemed to catch him off guard. He straightened his tie. "Would you believe Smith?"

His question of an answer tipped her to annoyed. "Smith. You don't say. What a coincidence, that's my name too."

"Really?"

She glared at him. "No." *Idiot.*

"Too bad." He sipped his remorse away. "Jaclyn Smith will forever be my favorite angel."

Mine too. "What's with the mystery, Mr. *Smith*?"

"I, um . . ."

Her silence spoke volumes while she waited for his response.

He shrugged, finally babbling out, "Well, I mean, you're here late. Really late. And you must frequent this bar regularly enough, because the bartender knows what you drink. And by how this all went down, I guess . . ." He ran a finger along the smooth edge of the bar and sucked in a breath. "I'm just not sure if you're, uh, a . . ."

She whipped her head toward him, her eyes blazing while he fumbled his explanation. "Oh my God. You think I'm a prostitute?"

More shrugging of his broad shoulders as he struggled to smile.

"Just to be clear, *unlike me*, I'm pretty sure a hooker would let anyone buy her a drink. In fact, the three of you would qualify under the call-girl definition of 'the more the merrier.'"

Richard actually seemed to blush. "No, of course not. I never imagined you were, um, a working girl. It's just that I'm, um—"

"Married?" she asked, disappointed. Though by the looks of his left hand, a ring had never graced his finger, as it was smooth. No signs of a tan line or indentation.

"No," he said with a slight huff of indignation. "I'm definitely not married. Look, I'm just digging the hole deeper, and as cool as our little scam has been, I've got to work in a few hours. I need to get going. How can I discreetly hand you half of this wad of cash before I head out?"

Oh, I'm not done playing with you, Mr. Smith.

He'd barely tugged the smooth leather wallet from his back pocket before she slid her hand around his forearm. Hopping off her bar stool, she energetically yanked him off of his.

"Oh, I know a way. And bring your drink."

With his newfound fortune, he left a C-note on the bar.

Leading him along, Jaclyn glued her body to his. It was nothing to fake a conversation punctuated with over-the-top giggles as they passed the two other men. Overtly flirting, she pressed her breasts against him as they strolled out to the lobby and toward the elevators. When the doors opened, she shoved herself against him, backing him inside.

The doors shut.

CHAPTER 3

Once the elevator doors closed, Jaclyn pressed the button for the twentieth floor of the West Tower, and promptly declawed herself from her full-on man attack.

Silence filled the small space as they were whisked upward. A chime announced their arrival. Richard stepped forward to exit, but she snatched his elbow, easing him back.

"Whoa there, cowboy." Again, she pushed a button, this time hitting the one for eleven. The doors closed. "In case your friends check the elevator, I want them to think we're going to my room. We're going to keep an eye out until they leave. I've got a great spot for spying."

"Somehow, I'm not surprised. And they're not my friends."

The doors opened to the famous eleventh floor "rooftop" pool. Touted in travel magazines as an architectural feat, the pool was nestled on a roof of a shorter tower, flanked by the taller twenty-story towers.

Round-the-clock access to the secluded venue offered a private oasis at the moment. Shimmers from the backlit water played perfectly against a backdrop of multicolored city lights and a warm, sweet-scented breeze.

They strolled to the far end of the inviting crystal-clear water, looking out over a glass half wall to the empty street below. Waiting on the undynamic duo's departure was taking forever. With a half-hidden yawn, Jaclyn plucked Richard's glass from his hand and poured his remaining bourbon into her lowball, then set his aside.

He smirked. "Sure, help yourself."

She sipped. "The last thing we need is you choking to death because you can't handle your booze. In a way, I'm saving your life."

He leaned an elbow on the glass railing, fully facing her. "You know, there's an old proverb that says if you save my life, you're entrusted to care for it."

Amused, she mirrored his stance. "Well, the way I heard it is if I save your life, you're now indebted to me for the rest of yours."

His eyes were pure playtime, teasing her with a knowing glance. "I'm actually prepared to accept your terms. Shall we put it in writing, back-of-the-napkin style, or are you as good as your word?"

"Oh, I'm so much better than my word." She tasted her drink, swallowing and letting the heat of the bourbon slide slowly down her throat.

Their gazes locked, and seconds ticked by.

Is he going to kiss me or what?

"So," Richard said, "are you sure they're not guests? Maybe they're going back to their rooms." He looked at his watch. "And as much as I'd love to grab a poolside chaise and glamp, I really do need to head out soon."

Guess not.

Lifting her gaze from his lips, she eyed him up and down. "I know they're not guests like I know you're not a guest, but for different reasons. Your pals were on an obvious late-night pub crawl, checking out the best Dallas bars have to offer, and the Joule is world renowned. They were wearing shirts with the same logo, for a convention that's hosted at the Gaylord. They've been taking their time going from one place to another, not overly drunk, but also not exactly sober. Trust me, they're not staying here."

Richard looked over the edge, studying the architecture of the pool overhanging the sidewalk below. Distracted by the anti-gravity feat, he seemed totally engrossed in something other than the hot-and-bothered woman standing inches from him.

Jaclyn wasn't sure he'd caught a single word she'd said until he asked, "What about me?" His dazzling blue gaze returned to her. "How do you know I'm not a guest?"

Echoes rose from the street below of men being a little too loud for two in the morning, and Richard and Jaclyn both popped their heads over the railing to see her prediction materialize. The men were leaving the hotel, still jovial, although they must have been kicked out after last call.

"See?" she said smugly. "Not guests."

Nodding, he conceded her point. "You were right. But you're probably used to that."

They exchanged smiles that promised more, and started walking slowly back toward the elevator.

"And me?" he asked.

"You? Take a look at yourself," she said, and he gave himself a quick once-over. "You're still in a suit and tie, likely burning the midnight oil. Then you decided to get away, maybe walk away to refocus. But thinking you'd be back quickly, you didn't bother changing into something casual, as if you're used to wearing suits like a second skin. And, if you were a guest, you would have gone somewhere else. My hunch is that hitting a bar wasn't exactly on your mind, because you don't strike me as the type to drink your way through a puzzle. Well, that and I've seen you drink."

Richard rolled his eyes at that.

"With your obvious workaholic tendencies, alcohol wasn't on your agenda, or you would've raided your own minibar and dove right back into whatever was bothering you. So, how'd I do?"

He unbuttoned his jacket and pocketed his hands. "I'm staying at the Crescent Court. But this crazy pool caught my eye when I drove in. It's not every day you see a pool hanging over a street midway up a hotel. I had to check the place out."

"At one in the morning?"

His lips lifted in a half smile. "I get restless, and I don't need much sleep. I like staying in big cities because wandering clears my head, and I can blend into the nightlife. You're right. I was trying to wrap my head around something. I happened to come in when those guys did, and, well, I saw you. We *all* saw you."

The deepening blue of his eyes held hers. "You said hello to the folks at the front desk, asking one of them how he was doing with a new baby in the house."

His endearing grin spread a little wider. "Then you made your way to the basement bar, and, looking the way you looked at this hour, we couldn't exactly not follow you. They noticed me noticing you and proposed a friendly bet. Worst-case scenario, I paid a high price for a little entertainment. But I figured I had nothing to lose. I was pretty sure you weren't falling for one of them. And if you did, I probably dodged a bullet." When she gave him an admonishing look, he shrugged. "Come on, you met them."

Truth.

"And best-case scenario?" She skated her fingers back and forth across the railing.

"Well, the wad of cash wasn't terrible," he said jokingly, and she was too charmed to be peeved. "That and I'd get to spend one of my first days in Dallas getting to know a beautiful fellow insomniac."

"So beautiful that you gave me an alias when you were perfectly teed up to hand me your business card," she said, raising her brows.

He gave her a sardonic smirk. "Yeah, why would anyone need an alias around a woman who looks the way you do, and just swindled a couple of strangers out of two grand?"

"I did no such thing." Pretending to be offended, she tapped his chest. "You did all the swindling. I just sat there."

He hung his head for a second, chuckling. "Fair enough. I guess you were just my con-artist life coach. Anyway, I wasn't sure if it was a good idea if we, well, continued—"

"Our mad partnership of crime and mayhem? Fine, I'll start my syndicate solo. Two thousand dollars *and* you got to buy me a drink. Clearing your head seems to be working for you."

She could only hold his gaze for a few seconds before he looked away.

"Oh, speaking of . . ." He pulled out his wallet and fumbled to remove their take, diligently separating it from the cash he came in with.

Jaclyn had just enough time to sneak a peek at the name on his driver's license encased in a clear plastic pocket of his wallet. Reluctantly, she stepped to the elevator and pushed the UP button as he counted the money.

He handed her half. "Here you go. For whatever it's worth, thank you. This was unexpected. And fun."

She eyed the money indifferently, then clasped her hands around his, securing the loot in his grip. "It's yours."

His intrigued baby blues fixed on her as a ping sounded, announcing the arrival of the elevator.

"The pleasure was all mine, Richard. Richard *Austin*." In a final impetuous act to close out their antics, she stole a swift, deep kiss.

His arms had barely molded around her before she pulled away. Admiring the bright red stain now covering his lips, she giggled. His wide-eyed fascination was priceless.

Damn, I'd love to bring Luke Skywalker to the dark side.

She stepped into the elevator and turned to him, sipping her stolen bourbon as the elevator doors closed. A smile tipped up her lips as she watched him standing with his mouth agape, still holding out his cash-filled hand.

~

Download the first book in the Ruthless Billionaires Club.
Available on All Platforms! **Get RUTHLESS GAMES Now>>>**

~

Need another fix of steamy suspense? The hot and steamy ALEX DRAKE SERIES with Alex, Madison, and Paco Robles is available on Amazon! **Get ACCESS Now>>>**

When seclusive billionaire Alex Drake sets his sights on Madison, obsession takes over. Unlocking his world was easy. Seducing her was inevitable. But securing her heart might be impossible. He's ready to give in to her every desire except for one. The only thing she wants. An answer. To a tiny question. Why her?

Get ACCESS Now>>>

∽

Join Lexxi's VIP reader list to be the first to know of new releases, special prices, and get freebies every week on all platforms!

Free hot romances & happily ever afters delivered to your inbox.
https://www.lexxijames.com/freebies

Rising
A Sinful Soldier Romance
Copyright © 2021 Lexxi James, Ltd. All rights reserved.
www.LexxiJames.com

Editing by
Pam Berehulke
Bulletproof Editing

Independently Published

Cover by Book Sprite, LLC.

No part of this publication may be reproduced, distributed, or transmitted in any form or by any means, including photocopying, recording, or other electronic or mechanical methods, without the prior written permission of Lexxi James, Ltd. Under certain circumstances, a brief quote in reviews and for non-commercial use may be permitted as specified in copyright law. Permission may be granted through a written request to the publisher at LexxiJamesBooks@gmail.com.

This is a work of fiction. Names, characters, places, and incidents are the product of the author's imagination. Specific named locations, public names, and other specified elements are used for impact, but this novel's story and characters are 100 percent fictitious. Certain long-standing institutions, agencies, and public offices are mentioned, but the characters involved are wholly imaginary. Resemblance to individuals, living or dead, or to events which have occurred is purely coincidental. And if your life happens to bear a strong resemblance to my imaginings, then well done and cheers to you! You're a freaking rock star!

ABOUT THE AUTHOR

Lexxi James is a USA Today bestselling author of romantic suspense. Her feats in multi-tasking include binge watching Netflix and sucking down a cappuccino in between feverish typing and loads of laundry.

She lives in Ohio with her teen daughter and the sweetest man in the universe. She loves to hear from readers!

www.LexxiJames.com/books

Printed in Great Britain
by Amazon